I0684536

Choices & Consequences

L. HUNTER

Choices and Consequences

Copyright © 2014 by L. Hunter

ISBN 978-0-9885056-4-3

Publisher: Word on da Street Publishing
Email: llperry803@gmail.com
Website: www.wordondastreetpublishing.com

Book Cover Design: Donna Osborn Clark at CreationByDonna.com

Editor: Timothy G. Green at Inkaissance: inkaissance@gmail.com

Typeset & Interior Design: www.CreationByDonna.com

Word on Da Street Publishing
Norcross, GA 30093

This book is dedicated to my mother Susan Hunter whose mind was just as creative as my own. "It's in the gene pool," as she would say.

Acknowledgments

Apart from the efforts of myself, the success of any project depends largely on the encouragement and support of others. I take this opportunity to express my gratitude to the people who have been instrumental in the successful completion of my book project. I would like to sincerely thank my Publisher/Agent/Promoter and now friend Lisa Tyrrell Perry-Amos of Word On Da Street Publishing. She believed in me from day one and for a million thanks wouldn't be enough. She was always literally a phone call away. Lisa always said I gotcha back and she did and still does for that I thank you.

Thank you, Donna Osborn Clark for an awesome book cover. You did your thing and I appreciate you for your time and effort.

To my CKFM fam we started out as strangers and grew to become lifelong friends. Thanks for not telling when I sat in the janitor's closet and the offices working on my book. Thank you for taking a interest in everything I wrote and hungered for more. Just know even if I don't talk you guys every day you all are on my mind.

To my DIA fam what do I say you guys are something else in a good way. We have laughed so hard together; we have talked about everything under and over the sun (smiling). I enjoyed working with you guys and thank you for supporting my book project and my crazy self.

Anthony J Dobbins thank you for staying up late nights with me working on this book project and always pushing me to think outside the box, listening to me read and reread scenes and for showing me how to edit. I appreciate you in more ways than I can say.

My thanks and appreciations also go to my children: LaKara, LaKrystal, Jalen, Jalissa and Joi. Thank you for being my personal cheer team always, understanding why I had to spend long hours at the computer, for cooking and making me pots of coffee while I worked on this project. We are all we got. I love you guys beyond human understanding.

Unfortunately I was unable to list everyone personally. But know you are in my heart and I thank you.

No one walks alone on the journey of life, I shall always remember those that joined me and followed beside me and stuck with me through thick and thin. Thank you all for making this possible with your encouragement and support.

Last but definitely not in the least for he is bigger than us all. I thank God for each blessing that he has given me, that he has placed people in my life to stand with me on this journey. I thank God for the opportunity to share my words with the world.

Chapter 1

Eighteen-year-old Jazmine Jaz Taylor was raised in Detroit. She was the only child born to James and Nicollet Taylor. They both were cross-addicted between cocaine and alcohol. Jaz never really knew her father. He was the fly by night sperm donor; as far as the family was concerned. Nicollet had died from a drug overdose when Jaz was 16. Over the next two years, she lived with her aunt Lola, whom was the only sister of Nicollet. Lola lived in a beautiful home in Palmer Park Woods, along with her husband Ron, and daughter Eve. Eve was the same age as Jaz. Things had been rocky ever since Jaz had come to live with them. Eve never failed in attempting to make Jaz feel like a charity case. This often meant that the two came to blows, which didn't make things easier for Jaz. Lola looked at her like a troublemaker and Ron watched her in his own perverted way every chance he got. Jaz never spoke of it; feeling Lola would never believe her anyway. Everything changed for Jaz one Thanksgiving Day.

The family had gathered at Nana's house for Thanksgiving dinner. Nana was the mother of Lola, Nicollet and Kevin. Kevin was the youngest and Jaz's favorite uncle. Nana lived on Boston, also in Detroit. Her home was a large colonial decorated with what Jaz referred to as *old people's stuff*, along with hand carved woodwork throughout the house. As dinner arrived to the dining table, they all gathered. Lola centered the table with her every year brown and orange paper turkey, which was horrendous to Jaz. Every time Jaz walked by the table, she thought to herself, *'Look at that ugly ass turkey.'* However, a smile came over her face when she saw the table being set with all the fixings of a Thanksgiving dinner. Nana put both feet in when she cooked. She was born and raised in Arkansas; arriving to the D when she was 21. She married Jack Taylor, Jaz's' grandpa, who passed years ago. Jaz loved hearing Nana's stories of growing in the south.

She could not wait to sit, eat, and get up. She loathed all the babbling, as if life was so perfect. The only comfort she felt was sitting and talking to her Nana. The Taylor family had created a family tradition to go around the Thanksgiving table and tell one thing they were thankful for that year. Every since Nicollet had passed, Jaz's answer had been the same each year. She was only thankful for her Nana.

This year was no different and every year Lola gave her the evil eye, as if to say *you ungrateful little bitch.*

Nevertheless, Jaz didn't care. After about an hour of eating and idle chitchat, Nana excused herself from the table to go upstairs and lie down. Soon everyone began clearing the table and putting up the food. Ron turned on some music and set it low, being careful not to disturb Nana. Kevin made drinks for the men company, while the women were in the kitchen cleaning and talking about issues they had with their husbands, boyfriends, children and anything else they could bitch about.

Kevin whispered over to Ron and the two of them slipped down to the basement unnoticed. After a few minutes, Jaz decided to go down and explore her curiosity. She spotted them smoking weed in a small room at the back of the basement. When Ron noticed Jaz peering into the room, he choked so hard that smoke bellowed out of his mouth. Kevin laughed until he too was choking.

"What you doing down here lil cuz? You try'na hit this?" Kevin continued laughing, while passing Jaz the blunt. Ron frowned.

"It's cool man; she ain't gonna say shit. Ain't that right lil cuz?" Kevin tests.

"I don't know what you talking about." Jaz smiled. She stepped in and closed the door behind her. Jaz didn't smoke but her *wanna be grown ass* attitude made her wanna try. One pull on the blunt and Jaz bent over choking hard as ever. Kevin got behind her and patted her back.

"Leave this to the big dog's lil girl," Ron laughed. Jaz looked up at him with an evil eye. She couldn't stand his ass. Next thing she knew, Kevin was placing his hand over her mouth aggressively.

"What the fuck man!" Ron said nervously.

"Shit! She owes me. Nigga you don't know how many times I done saved her ass coming up!"

Kevin retorts. Jaz tried to kick and scream but it was useless.

"Grab her fucking legs man; she kicking the shit outta me!" Kevin demanded. Ron did as was directed.

"I'm first, shit. I repeat; she owes me." Kevin continued, as his grip tightened over her mouth. Nervously, Ron began to fondle her breast through her blouse.

"What the fuck Ron!"

"Huh?" Ron mumbled his hands shaking.

"Rip that mutha fucker off man… damn!" Again, Ron did as was commanded, except this time more willingly. Flipping her breast out and over the front of her bra, Ron sucked at them hard while he wrestled to pull her jeans and underwear down. Tears streamed down Jaz's face; her heart was racing. She couldn't believe this was happening. The uncle she trusted and confided in, the only other person in her life she counted on besides Nana, was doing this to her. She tried to hold her legs closed with all her strength. Kevin flung her body to the hard floor. She could feel the cold cement on her backside as her jeans came down. Ron couldn't wait as his fingers forced their way inside her. Her body stiffened as she tightened her eyes. She felt nauseated. Her skin felt as if it were crawling.

Kevin directed Ron to hold her mouth closed while he climbed on top of her. He never looked her in the eyes or even touched her like Ron did; as if it made a difference. It seemed like forever as they took turns raping her. Jaz could hear Lola's voice calling out to her. She never thought she'd be relieved to hear her voice, until now.

They heard Lola too as they rushed to get their self together and slipped upstairs. They left Jaz on the cold basement floor. She felt as if her insides had been ripped out, but not before Kevin threatened her. Jaz laid there for a few moments after they left. Slowly and painfully, she got up. She managed to go to the laundry room and find one of her shirts that she had previously left. Hurting emotionally, mentally and physically, she slips past everyone and headed upstairs to the bathroom. Thinking to herself, *if I tell Lola, she won't believe me. She would find a way to make it my fault and that might kill my Nana.*

6

Choices and Consequences

Once upstairs she walked slowly down the hallway. The incident played over and over in her head. Going past Nana's room, she quietly peeked in. Nana was lying down, and her back to the door. Jaz heard the creeping of the old wooden stairs. Someone was coming. She quietly rushed to the bathroom. Nana gradually turns to the door, but no one was there. She situated herself in bed. Suddenly, Kevin appeared at the doorway of her room. Nana turned more abruptly this time.

"Kevin. How long have you been at my door? Her voice said, in a startling manner.

"I'm sorry Nana. I didn't mean to startle you but I came to see if you needed anything?" he said with guilt in his demeanor.

"No thank you; son. Where is Jaz? I want to see her before they leave."

"Oh I think she went to see Max… but I'll let her know," he added, as he looked down the hall at the closed bathroom door.

Meanwhile, Jaz washed and washed, repeatedly. The pain felt unbearable as she cried quietly. Looking in the mirror, she felt as if she was no longer herself. Brushing her hair and pulling it

7

into a ponytail, she proceeded to get dressed. She was now an innocent child, forced to be a woman.

A wrath rose up in her from deep inside. Yet calmly, she opened the bathroom door. Her face was completely void of expression. She headed downstairs to the kitchen. By now, everyone was in the living room, music still playing as they drank and lolly gagged. Jaz stood at the bottom step as her eyes scoured the room for Kevin and Ron.

"LOLA!" she screamed angrily. Suddenly everyone's attention turned to Jaz. Lola looked too.

"Who the hell you yelling at?" she answered angrily, not caring what the reason was. Jaz drew a deep breath.

"Ron and Kevin raped me!" She cried out, as her eyes filled with tears of hate.

"What!" Ron said angrily; attempting to disguise the guilt.

"Look Lola, me and Ron was downstairs smoking. Jaz asked to hit the blunt a few times and I told her no. Now she comes up here with this bullshit... Hell naw it ain't going down Jaz!" Kevin intervenes while staring at Jaz.

8

"Kevin you know you not supposed to be smoking in mommas' house and Ron... You just stupid right!" Lola fussed at Kevin and Ron. *Was this her only concern smoking in Nanas' house? What about me?* Jaz thought to herself. This made her blood boil even more; especially now. Everyone was looking at her as if she were the liar. She couldn't take it anymore. She reached for the fireplace poker stick and began swinging, striking Kevin first. Blood immediately gushed from his left cheek.

Ron knew he was probably next as he tried to stand before Jaz got to him. Jaz released a backswing and caught him on the right side of his temple. Before he could even clutch his face, he grabbed her by the throat with both hands and began choking her.

As everyone rushed to get Ron off Jaz, Nana came downstairs without uttering a single word. Things soon came to a halt when they noticed her. The apologies started flowing from every mouth in the room.

"What in the Lords name is going on here?" Nana said raising her voice just enough to be heard.

"Ron, why did you have your hands around this child's neck?" Nana's voice roared authority without raising her voice. Ron didn't say a word as he held a napkin against his head that one of the neighbors had handed to him.

"Mama everything's ok, things just got a little out of hand." Lola explained.

"Yes, well I can see that Lola." Nana said folding her arms.

"Nana, Kevin and Ron raped me in the basement and I want they ass locked up!" Jaz shouted as she ran to Nana and hugged her tight.

"What?" Nana said as she clutched her chest.

"See what you did you little bitch!" Kevin yelled.

"Mama," Lola called to Nana, as she fell to the floor still clutching her chest.

"Call 9-1-1 somebody, please! Girl if anything happens to my mama Im'ma kill you!" she shouted as she held Nana's head up.

Seeing Nana on the floor was too much. It seemed to be all her fault. Lola continued her insults.

"Get out!" Lola screams.

"You ain't gon be shit, just like yo junkie ass momma."

Jaz looked around the room while some stared at her in disbelief as others tended to Nana.

Chapter 2

"Why do you have to cause trouble Jaz?" Micah asked. He was a younger cousin of Jaz. Jaz eyes dropped to the floor. Bolting for the door, she ran and ran. Not knowing where she was running to, only what she was running from. Hours had gone by and she was now tired, cold and hungry. She was going to every gas station and restaurant that she could to keep warm. Soon managers were putting her out for not purchasing anything. She didn't know where she'd be sleeping. Max was her last hope.

It seemed as if everyone in the neighborhood had heard of what happened. She came across neighbors and people in the streets who heard. They all with heard a different version. None of it was what happened and Jaz didn't feel the need to explain.

She was told that her Nana was hospitalized via Mrs. Janie, a neighbor who worked in one of the gas stations. Jaz knew that Max would help her, even if it meant she would get in trouble for it. She didn't want to burden Max, but at this point, she had no choice. Heading to Max's house, she saw Max and her step dad Mr. Butler tussling in the doorway. He was trying to pull Max back into the house. Jaz noticed Mrs. Butlers' car was gone. She ran to the porch. Max was yelling and hitting Mr. Butlers' hands as she cursed him.

"I'm telling my mama you dirty ass old man! You like raping girls!" Max screamed. There it was that ugly word… "rape". Jaz too went "H.A.M." on Mr. Butler, hitting him in the face and anywhere else she could. Mr. Butler soon receded back into the house slamming the door.

"You ain't never getting ya black ass in here again!" he yelled thru the door. Max kicked the door as hard as she could.

"Fuck you! You dirty mutha fucka! Max screamed at the top of her lungs. Fuck him! She shouted as they walked off the porch. The two walked and walked for what seemed to be hours until they reached a Coney Island up on Livernois. Max knew Les worked there. Les was cool. She and Max knew some of the same people from the streets. They needed to get warm, eat and figure out their next move.

"Hey Jaz you got some ends?" Max asks as she searched her own pockets.

"Nope," Jaz responded shaking her head.

"Damn... that's alright. Les will hook us up." "So I heard about what happened at Nanas."

"Yea... which version did you hear?" Jaz frowned, with sadness in her voice.

"Come on; you know better than that. I know that was sum bullshit, but I got yo back." Max clarified with a grin while nudging at Jaz. Feeling relieved, Jaz knew there was no need to go into details. Walking into the Coney Island Max waved for Les to come over to the table where they sat.

"What's up Max and friend?" Les smiled.

"Oh this Jaz... Jaz this Les and she cool as hell; especially today." Max smirked while eyeing Les. Les knew that meant Max had no ends on the food.

"Hello," Jaz waved.

"Hello…" Les asked, pulling out her pad.

"Let me get a cheeseburger deluxe, chili on da fries and no cheese." Max ordered.

"I'll have the same," Jaz added.

"Okay be up in a minute or two," Les said walking away. After about five minutes, Les came back with their orders.

"Thank you." Jaz replied.

"You're very welcome." Les smiled and turned to Max.

"Max you should take some pointers from your friend." Les laughs as Max jokingly sticks her tongue out.

"Oh… Whatever!" Les joked waving Max off. "You crazy but you already know that right?" she added, as she walks away. Half way thru their meal Max got up and walked over to the counter; she flagged Les.

"Hey let me use your cell," she asks. After what looked like a few calls, she headed back to the table to finish her meal. Jaz didn't ask any questions but was curious. Therefore, she waited a few minutes. Finally, the suspense was killing her.

"Max!" Jaz grumbled as Max laughed. Max looks at Jaz for a moment with a half grin before answering.

"Yea…" Max continued to grin.

"Yea…" Jaz responds.

"You know curiosity killed the cat… right?" Max jokes.

"Yea well anyway… what we gonna do and who you call?" Jaz questioned.

"Relax, relax; one question at a time." Max put her hands up, as if she was being held up.

"Okay… I got this friend. He is so fine, he smell good, and he-"

"Max!" Jaz interrupted.

"Okay for real he is fine though. He gon pick us up in a few."

(*Honk Honk!*)

"Oh shit that's him come on." Max hurried Jaz.

"Good looking Les," Max gestured.

"Max wait is he…" Jaz hurried as she grabs the last of the fries off her plate.

"Yea he cool don't worry. I got us." Max said, trying to ease her mind. Jaz quickly waved bye to Les.

"Yall be careful." Les replied, as her eyes squint at the pearl white phantom awaiting them outside. Max climbed into the front while Jaz proceeded to the back.

"What up Dirk?" Max greeted proudly.

"What up doe. Who is shorty in da back?" Dirk asks as he motions his head toward Jaz. Before Max could say anything, Jaz spoke. "My name is Jaz, not shorty"

"Oh shit… I like that you got some fire huh… Well, okay Ms. Jaz." Dirk laughs.

"You aight wit me?" Dirk added, while nodding his head as he continued to drive and taking occasional glances back at Jaz, as she ignored them. However, she thought to herself, *he is fine with that reddish brown skin and tapered fade; damn.* They rode for what seemed to be like an hour, as the scenery began to change. She knew she was far from the hood.

They ended up in Beverly Hills. She didn't even know there was a Beverly Hills in Michigan.

They arrived at a high-rise building that looked like floors of lofts on a gorgeous street that was aligned with pink blossom trees.

"Damn nigga! You straight sold the hood out huh?" Max jokes.

"Shit this big money out here baby girl. It was time to move up." He added, as they exited the car.

Walking through a corridor of elegance fountains and plants, expensive furniture in the lobby, you would've thought rich people stayed here.

They went up to the 21st floor and the elevator opened up to his living room. *Damn this is live*, Jaz thought to herself as she continued to keep her cool. The walls were painted a deep dark red; trimmed with white and beautiful cherry wood floors. The kitchen adorned with brown and black granite counter tops, with a black finish on the cabinets, not to mention matching marble floor. This dude was not skimping on the décor. Hell, it even had an upstairs with a winding black staircase.

"Have a seat and make yourselves comfortable," he welcomed them.

"Thank you." Jaz replied, as she sat down on the end of the custom-made Black Italian leather sofa   that sat in front of a large plasma screen on the wall.

"Okay, I wanna take a shower. Is that cool D?" Max said, as she tugged at her clothes.

"Yea up the stairs to your left, fresh towels in the closet to the right." he added. Max headed upstairs to shower, almost instantaneously. Dirk sat as close to Jaz as he could. Checking her out, his eyes wandered to her breasts that were small but full and round. Her legs were formed to perfection. She had those childbearing hips people talk about; thick thighs, and ass for days, which he'd already noticed when she got out the car.

"You got some pretty ass skin. You part Indian or summin'?" Dirk inquired, as he continued to stare. Jaz instantly laughs. She has heard that so many times growing up and it sounded even sillier coming from him, even though it was true.

"Ah... is that a smile?" he joked. Jaz stopped smiling and frowned.

Choices and Consequences

"Hey don't frown, you even prettier when you smile. Dirk leaned in to get a good look at her face.

"Naw, I'm serious. You got a natural beauty bout you... seriously." he compliments.

"Thank you." Her voice softens. Max came down the stairs with her long black hair still damp from the shower. She pulled it into a ponytail. Walking over to Jaz, she nudges her.

"Your turn Ms. Thang." Jaz didn't say a word as she stood to head upstairs. Anything she could do to wash the stench off of her from Ron and Kevin she'd gladly do. 100 washes probably wouldn't help. Max joined Dirk on the couch. She always had a major crush on him but always knew she would never be his main girl; partly because he had her by at least 5 years. Never the less, she didn't care.

Once Max heard the bathroom door close, she began caressing Dirk's left thigh. He smiled. That gave Max the ok to proceed and she did. Max slid down between his legs, slowly unzipping his jeans. His manhood intensified as he slunk down opening his legs. He moaned. His hands scuffling to free his hardness, Max strokes it with her tongue.

21

"Damn Max," he whispered. She looks up at him and smiles.

Before long, her mouth submerged his hardness. Her mouth was warm and wet. Her hands gently stroked the shaft of his dick. She licked his balls, which made him groan. Dirk started rolling her nipples between his thumbs and index finger, which drove her crazy. As her mouth got wetter, the sensation between her thighs grew stronger.

By now, Jaz was standing at the top of the balcony. Feeling a lump in her throat, she thought, *'Why would Max do this, especially after everything that's happened?'* Dirk started to moan louder and louder until he came. Max continued to drain him. He was in awe at the sight of her swallowing his warm liquid. Once he finished, Max got up and went to the kitchen.

Dirk stood up and got himself together. Shaking his head, he smiled.

"Shit Max, what you need?" he laughs.

"Well since you asked, we need a place to stay for a minute, some clothes, you know... shit like that," she replied.

"Tell you what... Im'ma look out. But ya'll gotta get ya'll shit together. Go to school, whatever. In the meantime, I got you... Shiid... as long as you doing what you just did on a regular. We can do this!" Dirk laughs, as he headed upstairs bypassing Jaz. She felt sick as she came down the stairs. She hurried to the kitchen where Max was and grabbed her arm.

"Is there anywhere else we can stay Max?" Jaz pleaded.

"Look I got us; stop worrying. I ain't stayin' nowhere I ain't wanted or squatting in a shit hole of a house. Oh... well there is the shelter... you wanna go there?" Max was now sarcastic and agitated. Jaz said nothing as she shakes her head and walks away. Max soon went to her.

"Hey... you're my best friend. Anyways, I just wanta stay here. Look at this place. It beats anywhere else. Jaz I got us... feel me?" Max attempted to make light of the situation.

"Yea Max but..."

"No butts Jaz, we don't have to worry about shit. No clothes, no food, no money and anything else we want. Just let me worry about the details okay… please?" Max reassured.

"Alright," Jaz surrendered. She headed back to the couch feeling defeated, knowing at some point, the details of this bullshit would come to a head.

Dirk came down in a navy blue pinstripe Dolce and Gabbana button up, with matching blue slacks and Cartier cologne. He was known for being sharp in the hood and out here it was no different if not more so.

Placing a 100-dollar bill on the buffet table, he grabs his keys. "Ladies there's money for food. You can go out or order in. It's a lot of restaurants out here, oh and here's a card. Dis my man's Cash. He'll drive you anywhere you need to go… just call him," he added, as the elevator opened. Max walked over to the table picking up the card and money.

"A fuckin' driver! Jaz… a fucking driver!" she screamed jumping on Jaz playfully.

"Okay, okay, okay!" Jaz laughs. They ordered in Chinese food and watched movies until falling asleep on the couch.

Chapter 3

A year had passed. Max was now 20 and Jaz, just 19. Dirk and Max were an item now, something Max never thought would happen. Jaz now enrolled into a community college as a Business Administration Major. Unfortunately, the lifestyle had taken control over Max. She started snorting cocaine and drinking heavily. Jaz knew this was not the life she wanted for herself. Max was literally out of control and even sexing anyone Dirk told her to. Jaz argued with her repeatedly. She told her someone who loves you wouldn't want to share you with everybody. Continuously she begged Max to get away from there with her. Nevertheless, Max wouldn't hear of it and Jaz wouldn't leave without her.

Finally, Jaz started saving the money Dirk was giving them to shop. Jaz had a plan to one-day leave and hoped that at that time her friend Max would leave with her. But, she kept it all to herself until the time came.

One night Jaz came in from class. It had to be about 10 p.m. The place was a mess. Dirk was stretched out on the couch and Max was upstairs, Jaz assumed. They must have had a long day. 10 o'clock was a little early for these two to be sleep.

Jaz headed upstairs to check on Max, and then went to shower before heading back downstairs to clean up. After her shower, there she was downstairs picking up their mess as usual. There were empty bottles of Tequila and take-out food containers everywhere. Dirk jumped up with his gun in his hand.

"Dirk, wait it's just me!" Jaz shouted, with her hands up fearing he would accidentally shoot her.

"Damn Jaz, I could've killed you! What the hell you doing?" he woke up, from his drunken sleep.

"I'm trying to clean up. It's a mess down here." her voice shaky. Dirk slowly got up attempting to help clean.

Choices and Consequences

"How was class?" he asked, as he moved in closer.

Jaz responded. Dirk leaned his back against the kitchen island as his eyes watched her. He always had feelings for her but never voiced it, feeling like he'd only corrupt her as he did Max. That was partly the reason for keeping Max around. He knew if Max stayed that Jaz would too.

As Jaz passes by, he got a whiff of the strawberry scent in her curly hair, which extended halfway down her back. The color was a sandy blond that complimented her smooth caramel skin; void of imperfections. Dirk continued to gaze. He wanted Jaz so bad that he could feel his heart pounding as his hardness grew. She felt his eyes on her as she tried to pick up faster. He moved in closer and closer to her.

(*BUZZ*)

"Damn!" he grumbled as if it interrupted him. Jaz thought to herself, '*Saved by the buzzer.*' Dirk walked over to the intercom.

"Yeah…" Dirk answered a bit agitated.

"Dirk let me up, it's Damon," the husky voice yelled back. Dirk smiles. "My man's D money…

Hell Yea!" Dirk hit the elevator button. Damon was one of the only real friends Dirk had left. Everyone else wanted something from him. Damon and Dirk grew apart as adults but remained friends. Damon had moved to Atlanta a few years back to pursue his dreams of playing in the NFL, but a knee injury put those dreams on hold. Therefore, he decided to go for his MA in business. The elevator doors opened and the two hugged and wrestled each other as if they were kids again.

"What brings you back dog; all up in Hotlanta and shit? Last time I heard yo ass was up in Georgia Tech nigga." Dirk adds.

"Yeah well, my mom's sick man. So you know I had to come back." Damon looked sad just saying it.

The two continued talking and Jaz continued cleaning up. She also continued taking quick glances at Damon. His black hair was faded with precision, along with the trim goatee and mustache that lined his perfectly full lips. Damon was 6'2. A complexion of honey; his eyes hazelnut tone and his laid-back style only complimented his swag. Jaz was feeling him too much, too early and knew it was time for her to go, but bypassing the two of them was not happening.

"Hey Jaz, I know you gotta go study, but this my man's D money that I told you and Max about." Dirk introduces. Jaz extended her hand to his and Damon obliges her.

"Just Damon… Nice to meet you Jaz." he smiled. She smiled.

"Same here, but I do need to study you know how it is." She added referring to those college days.

"Oh Fo sho," Damon remembers.

"Well… Goodnight fella's." She hurried waving her hand.

"Goodnight." They both spoke in unison as they watched her up the stairs. Damon smiles and looks at Dirk.

"Damn man, it's like that huh?" Damon asked.

"Yea you know how I do." Dirk laughed.

"Well, look I'll hit you up tomorrow. I'll be in town for a minute." Damon said, as he pressed the elevator button.

"Aight D money." Dirk laughed, as he gave him dap.

Over the next few weeks, Damon and Dirk hung like wet rags. Damon spent a couple nights out of the week hanging with Dirk, until he got the call that his mom was moved to the intensive care unit. Damon's visits became few to non-existent. Dirk stayed at the hospital with him up until his business called him away. He ended up sending Jaz to stay with Damon at the hospital in his place. Max was always off doing whatever, as she always did. This continued for about three months.

Meanwhile, Damon and Jaz became closer and closer; physically, emotionally and mentally. Now was not the time to act on it. Damon taught Jaz how to drive in the hospital parking lot. Dirk always had a driver for her and Max, so they had no need to drive. Damon and Jaz had lunch together every day at the hospital.

A month later, unfortunately, Damon's mom pasted away. Dirk paid for all funeral expenses. Days after the funeral, Dirk and Damon seemed to be hanging out more than usual which meant Jaz saw less and less of Damon. She continued going to class. Thanksgiving was nearing. The thought of what happened back at Nanas weighed heavy on her. However, it came and went. Friday night Jaz didn't have class so she agreed to go out with the crew for appearances sake.

They went to club Babylon in downtown Detroit. All eyes were on them as they walked in. Free Thinkerz Ink was showcasing and Dirk knew their manager. Dirk and Damon came into the club, canvassed the club conversing, mingling, and then the drinking had begun. They left Max and Jaz at a table with drinks, which didn't last very long.

"You drinking that or you gonna stare at it?" Max asked sarcastically, pointing at the drink in front of Jaz. Jaz took a deep breath and shook her head as she slid the tall blue drink over to Max. After a few drinks, Max got up. "I'll be back. Sit tight and mingle, shit. Do somethin' wit yo square ass." Max shouted over the music. Stumbling over her own feet, she headed to the VIP room.

After about thirty minutes later, Jaz went to find Max. There she was in the VIP room with two of the rappers and an unknown female. Eyes were on Max as the door swung open and back closed. As she peered thru the small opening, she caught Dirk and Damon in her sight. She then entered the VIP.

Max was giving head to one of the rappers while the other rapper was fucking her from behind. Not to mention, the unknown chick was giving Max head. Jaz was furious and appalled. There was nothing she could do anymore. Max had turned into this person a long time ago. Instead of arguing with Max, she figured she'd rather have her in her life, than not at all.

Chapter 4

A month later, Thanksgiving had come and went like a regular day. Damon came full circle with Dirk and his business transactions. He had his hands in damn near every deal. He even had connections from out of the country. He was Dirks business partner in every sense of the word. Max was getting on Dirks last nerve. He grew tired of her. If it were not for Jaz being there, he probably would have kicked her ass out a long time ago. Even though he and Jaz were not on that level, he wanted to keep her around.

Christmas was now around the corner. Jaz and Max were home alone and Jaz put up the tree. Max was supposed to help but she sat her lazy ass on the couch drinking and running off at the mouth. Dirk and Damon walked in with some hood rat who presumed, she was classy.

"Jaz, Max... this is Mo," Dirk introduced.

"Hello." Jaz spoke.

Mo returned the greeting. Max looked at her but didn't say a word. That was the first night things began to get worse in the place they called home. Dirk was high. There is a rule never get high on your own supply and Dirk broke it. Max was already pissed with him because he had stopped spending time with her.

"What the fuck is wrong with you Max? You can't speak. Oh, but you can open yo mouth to suck another niggas dick right!" Dirk shouted. Max's facial expression said it all before she even opened her mouth. Instead, she laughed it off, got up and refilled her drink. Damon stood staring at Jaz until Dirk walked over to Max at the kitchen island. Dirk walked up behind Max, grabbing a fistful of hair and snatching her head back.

"Who the fuck you laughing at; huh?" He shouted in her face. Max just looked at him with a devious smirk on her face. She knew how to fuck with him and Jaz hated it. She knew Max was in a fuck wit him mood and it wouldn't be good.

Choices and Consequences

"Dirk, please stop." Jaz pleaded as she walked over to the two of them with tears in her eyes. He looked at her. She seemed to always be the calm to his storm. Because of the way he felt for her he released the back of Max's head and walked away. He poked her hard at her forehead with his index finger.

"You lucky… Jaz was here to save yo ass." He said, as he walked away to pour himself a drink. Max sips the drink she had previously poured.

"What the fuck you mean Jaz saved me?" You fucking both of us… and this new bitch… huh? Max said sarcastically. It didn't take long before Dirk reached over and smacked the shit out of Max.

It was on now and they began fighting. Damon and Jaz attempted to break it up. Dirk punches Max repeatedly in the face as if she were a man.

"Dirk! What the fuck!" Damon yells. He didn't condone hitting women. Jaz cried out in a panic.

"Please! Let her go… Please Dirk!" Dirk looked up at Jaz as tears flowed from her eyes. She was hurt in her face. Looking down at Max bleeding

35

on the floor, he was embarrassed at what he'd done. He got up calmly and retreated upstairs… slamming the door behind him.

"Look Mo I'm taking you home. Jaz you take care of Max. I'll be back soon as I can." Damon instructed, as he and Mo left. Jaz got a paper towel and wet it in attempt to clean the blood from Max's face. Dirk called out to Max. As she went to get up, Jaz whispered.

"No."

"Listen every couple has their ups and downs Jaz." She responded, as she went to him anyway.

'I am done with this shit,' Jaz thought to herself, as she watched Max disappear upstairs. Jaz slumped down on the couch. *'I have to get the hell out of here,'* she continued to think.

Dirk came down walking toward her. He sat down so close she could smell the liquor on his breath. Licking his lips and taking in a deep breath he stares down at her breast.

"I'm sorry you saw that side of me," he tried to explain. Suddenly Max called down to him. "Baby, did you apologize?"

"Yea, just finishing up now," he yelled back. Dirk licked his lips once over and got up and went back to Max. Jaz proceeded to pick up the broken glass and ornaments. As a last ditch effort he walks over to Jaz.

"Don't worry I'll get some more Christmas stuff for you tomorrow." He said, before going off to Max. Afterward she was privileged to hearing irritating sexual noises from their room.

Subsequently, Jaz finished decorating the tree. '*This lil Charlie Brown tree is still beautiful*,' she thought to herself. Dirk had told her the day he bought it home that he only did it for her. Damon soon came in and saw Jaz sitting in the dark.

"You okay."

"I will be." Jaz answered.

"Hey, will you come take a ride with me?"

"A ride where?"

"I just wanta talk to you in private that's all… will you?" he requested. Jaz looks at him for a moment before going upstairs to change into her pink and black Baby Phat jogging suit. She slips on the matching BP boots. Jaz always had the knack for coordinating. Taking her time, Damon wondered if she was riding or playing him to the left.

"You ready?" she asked.

"Yeah, I thought you left me hanging for a minute." Damon laughs it off. They rode for about 30 minutes until arriving to the outskirts of Detroit. It was beautiful, with nicely cut lawns, and gorgeous homes. Arriving to a high-rise apartment building, they continued up to the 16th floor. Arriving at his apartment, Jaz couldn't believe it.

"Wow this is stunning... look at you!" Jaz pokes fun at him. "I would have never guessed... you'd think a woman decorated it."

"Thanks, my mom's taught me a lot," he laughs, with his hand on his chin trying to look debonair. "Care for anything to drink, eat?"

"No I'm okay but thank you anyway," Jaz added, as she sat down on the white leather sofa. Damon sat next to her staring at her for a moment.

"What's up? Why we here Damon?" she questioned. He took a deep breath not knowing what type of reaction he was about to get. A different look came over his face, gentler and inviting, since his mom passed. Clearing his throat, he stood up. Jaz reached for his arm.

"Please sit," she asks, slightly tugging at his arm. Damon sat, as his hands slid down his face. Turning he looks at Jaz.

"There's no easy way to say what I need to say Jaz." Damon expressed.

"Okay just say it… what is it?" She inquired.

"Look Jaz… I'm in love with you. You the only reason I stayed after my mom passed away." Tears began to form. He never felt like this… not this quick. Jaz had come to be his best friend.

She was the person who comforted him when his mom past and she were so easy to love. Damon quickly stood, pacing the room. It was quiet for a moment. He was nervous; his heart racing. Jaz stood and walked over to him. Gently, she lightly touched his eyes.

"I love you too." she looks up at him with a half-smile. Damon blew a hard breath as his eyes closed. He didn't know she felt like this. "What took you so long?" she asked.

Opening his still watery eyes, he looks down at this short beautiful woman standing before him; a woman who had his heart long before she knew it.

"Dirk made it seem like you and Max was his… and I know he done dat shit befo. Anyway, I was cool just being around you; even if that meant just a little time with you. That's why it…"

Jaz stop him in mid-sentence. Reaching up she hugged his neck, pulling him closer gently kissing his lips. Damon felt like his soul was on fire. As he returns her soft kisses, he paused.

"Damn uza a fine mufucka." He compliments. "You smart as hell, fun to be wit, understanding, caring… all the shit a nigga need. This ain't the life for us is it?"

Jaz shook her head in agreement, as her own tears filled her eyes.

"I need you Damon," she says, as he began to kiss her. This time, as his skillful tongue took more control exploring her mouth. Jaz could feel the tension rising in his jeans as she presses herself against him more. Her hands caressed his head, along with the back of his neck.

40

Damon picked her up and headed to the bedroom; his hands clutching the roundness of her ass. She softly moans. Without further a due, they slowly undressed each other admiring the other's flaws and all. Damon's hardness was aching to feel her.

Jaz's erect nipples screamed to be touched. He obliged, taunting one with his mouth and gently squeezing the other with his fingers, as he was being very mindful of giving each one the attention it deserves. Her body quivered at his touch. She never felt like this. She had never been in love. This was her only sexual experience other than the rape. Damon was gentle and took his time. He knew what she'd been through in the past.

His lips journeyed to her inner thighs, watching as he arrives to her sweetness. Placing her left leg over his shoulder, she balances herself with the assistance of the dresser. Damon's tongue soon was buried inside of her, darting in and out as his lips savored her wetness. Her legs tremble as her juices gushed. He enjoyed every drop. This was a surreal moment for the two of them. They never thought this could be, especially Jaz. Her moans became louder as she pulled his face deeper. Feeling the weakness in her legs, he decided it was now time. Picking her up Damon laid her on her back. She continued to hang on to his neck.

Taking a brief look at who laid before him, he took a deep breath. Even though his hardness was pulsating, he wanted this to last as long as possible. Easing between her already spread legs, Jaz embraced him as he moved smoothly inside her tightness. He gasps at the wetness of her, as she gasps at the fullness of him. His movements began faster and deeper, touching her core. Intense pleasure swept thru them. She came harder. Damon's movements intensified. Pulling her upward, she decided to straddle him, legs wrapped around his waist. She leaned back just enough for him to watch her breast bounce before him. He assisted with the ride, gripping her ass firmly. Moans filled the air as he called her name repeatedly. Their kisses were deep and passionate. Their movements came together in one rhythmic motion, until they slowed to a captivating climax. She laid her head on his chest. It was a place of calmness.

Chapter 5

Unexpectedly, a loud banging noise was at the apartment door that alarmed the two.

"Rest… it's okay," he told Jaz, as he got up and grabbed a pair of jogging pants off the chair. Jaz pulled the cover over her head and closed her eyes. Damon slipped on his house shoes and quietly pulled the bedroom door close.

He looked through the peephole letting out a sigh of disappointment. He cracks the door.

"What's up Max?"

"You seen Jaz? And don't say you haven't nigga!" Max woofs.

"Number one, relax your damn voice." Damon snapped.

"Look, I don't got time for this. Dirk been calling your phone nonstop and he looking for the both of ya'll." her voice lower but still irate. Damon allowed Max to come into the apartment.

"Have a seat Max," he said, feeling annoyed.

"Shit, don't be mad at me cuz yo boss looking fo yo ass." she laughed. She began to walk around the apartment snooping, while taking momentary glances at Damon. He went into the bedroom searching his jeans for his cell.

28 missed calls.

"Damn," he added as he continued scrolling through his phone. Jaz rolled over.

"Baby what's wrong?" Damon drew a deep breath, and then exhaled.

"Yo girl Max is out in the living room. She said Dirk looking for us. Baby this nigga called my phone 28 mutha-fucking times; 28!" Damon was furious but held it together. Jaz looked sad knowing this wouldn't turn out well. Damon walked around to Jaz's side of the bed and kneeled down.

"Will you leave with me today... right now? Jaz, you gonna have ta leave Max cause you know she ain't going nowhere anyway. Leave all this shit; start somewhere new... today, please Jaz." he pleaded. Surprisingly, she responded.

"When do we leave baby?" she asks, lightly stoking his face.

"Shit right now; get dressed." he added, while looking for his shirt.

Dirk continues to call Damon as he heads over to his place. *Dis bitch ass nigga ain't answering da phone? I know Jaz wit him. Im'ma fuck dis nigga up! (He snorts a line) I know she better answer her mutha fucking phone. I pay dat bill. I put dis nigga on.* He dials Jaz.

"Now he's calling me. Whatchu want me to do? Jaz asked frantically.

"Fuck dat nigga, let's go. Grab my keys." He ordered. All of a sudden, Max busted into the bedroom.

"Straight up… it's like that? You gon' leave a bitch hanging when I saved your mutha fucking life!" Max shouted.

"Max calm down, it's not like that. You want this life, not me. I asked you time and time again to leave but you wouldn't. I have to think about what I want… where my life is going… my happiness Max!" Damon didn't intervene because he knew Jaz could handle herself and figured it would be best if he stayed out of it. He went into the bathroom

45

leaving the two to hash it out. Jaz continued to search the room for her things while getting dressed. Max went on and on about what she did for Jaz and how Jaz think she's better than everyone else. Without warning, Dirk stood in the doorway of the bedroom as he listened to the ass end of the argument. He was tapping his right leg with his revolver.

"Go downstairs Max." he said calmly, as he stared at Jaz in disgrace. They were taken aback by the sight of him; not realizing that he'd slipped in. "So you gonna up and leave the nigga who took care of you right... to be with a nigga who got what he got from me? That is some stupid shit Jaz... and you suppose' to be the smart one... riiight?" he added.

Max stood there in silence. She knew in her heart that he always wanted Jaz, but only settled for her. Dirk yelled at her to go downstairs once again. She proceeded to do as told. As Max walked past the bathroom door, she noticed it was ajar. Damon's, 40 cal. was locked in on her and he motioned for Max to be quiet. Luckily for her, she did.

46

Jaz continued to stand her ground, staring at Dirk with defiance.

"Look, I always knew this wasn't the life for you. That's why I never pushed for you to do the shit Max, or any of us did. Jaz, I fucking love you!" Dirk expressed with insincere smoothness.

"Huh… you love me? Are you serious? She almost laughed rhetorically. You don't love anybody but ya damn self Dirk! You full of shit!" Dirk's smoothness turns to fury as he walks over and grabs Jaz by the neck. Her eyes turn livid. She thought to herself, *'this nigga got to be crazy to put his nasty hands around my neck.'*

"I see bitch… dis shit don't faze you huh?" he laughs. "But, I bet if I smack yo ass that'll get you right!" he yelled. Suddenly he felt the hard cold steel behind his neck.

"I don't think you wanna do dat son." Damon announced. He frisked Dirk. "You should've brought a bigger gun nigga." Dirk released his grip from Jaz as he shot her a wicked smirk.

"You know you outta pocket for this one right?" Dirk stated.

"It is what it is." Damon responded, as Jaz gathered the rest of her things. Dirk continued to smirk.

"You betta kill me right here, right now... if not you already kno' I'm coming fo dat ass." he laughs.

"I should just kill yo punk ass right now nigga." Damon had wrath in his voice as he backed down the hallway towards the living room. He held Dirk by the back of his shirt, 40 cal. still at the back of his neck. Jaz waited at the front door. Damon viewed over his apartment.

"Jaz, grab that duct tape from the kitchen drawer." he directed. Damon forced Dirk into a kitchen chair. "Tape his arms and legs to the chair. Damon took the butt of his gun and hit Dirk across the back of the head, enough to knock him out. He knew in his mind he needed to kill him cause Dirk was the kinda nigga that would not stop till his vengeance was won.

"Damon please; let's just please go!" she pleaded. Damon looks at her and back at Dirk she grabs his hand begging him to leave. They proceeded to his truck.

Choices and Consequences

Once Max seen Jaz and Damon fleeing, she said fuck it and went back in to find Dirk taped up. She freed him. "Baby... Baby…" Max cried. Dirk shook his head, opened his eyes and saw Max. He stumbled to get up, pushing her out of the way and saying nothing as he bolted for the door. He grabbed a 9mm he'd kept under the seat. Dirks jealousy and frustration ate at him. The whole ordeal played like a movie in his head while he drove, which added fuel to the fire. He left Max to tend for herself.

He rode around till nightfall smoking, drinking, and sniffing. Nothing could coat the feeling. He arrived to Cash's apartment at Lafayette Place on the eastside. Cash was Dirks number one soldier. Cash did anything for Dirk, even killed on gp. Dirk called him letting him know he was outside.

"Come on up my nigga." Cash spoke through the intercom as he buzzed Dirk up.

"Fa sho." Once inside, Dirk immediately poured himself a shot of Absolute straight. It didn't take Cash long to figure out the nature of the visit.

49

"What up D… who we gotta get cuz you know I don't give a fuck my nigga!" Cash makes it clear, as he pulls out matching Berettas, one in each hand. "Shit I'm like John fucking Wayne in this bitch. Nigga you know me!" he laughs. That made Dirk smile.

"Yea, I know you a true soldier," he laughed, downing his drink and pouring another. Dirk sat down on the gray cloth sofa and threw back the drink he'd just made. He went on to tell Cash what happened with Damon, leaving out a few details.

"I knew that nigga had anotha' muthafucking agenda… I knew dat shit!" Cash made some phone calls, as did Dirk. About 20 minutes later a slew of Dirk and Cash soldiers stood outside awaiting orders. Dirk and Cash met up with them and gave instructions. Not long after, cars and trucks sped off in every direction searching for Jaz and Damon. Throughout the night, they hunted. Anyone driving a pearl white Range Rover got it bad if Cash felt they wasted his time. Dirk soon went home, sending everyone else home too. Cash decided he would get higher and pursue the task at hand.

Choices and Consequences

Around three o'clock a.m. Dirk got up and went downstairs. Max was just turning over. He was on the phone. Max laid there eaves dropping.

"Yea Gray, it's Dirk. Man, I'm calling in dat debt now my nigga. Yea, find this bitch ass nigga Damon… Damon Hicks… Yea that's him. He'll be with Jaz… Yea, yea my Jaz. Take him to the warehouse and bring her to me. Bet!" (*Hangs up*)

Max knew this was bad. Even though she and Jaz fell out, she wouldn't give Dirk the satisfaction of touching Jaz. She didn't care about Damon. Max got up and went downstairs as if she didn't overhear. Walking over in an attempt to hug Dirk, he nudges her away.

"I ain't feelin that shit right now… Damn!"

"What… you ain't feelin it? Why you still looking for them? He don't wanna be here and she don't want your ass no way." Max said spitefully. Dirk frowned thinking to himself, '*Looking for them… how the fuck she know? Dat bitch was ear hustling.*'

All of a sudden Max felt a sharp pain across her face that made her eyes water. Dirk had backhanded her, leaving imprints of his rings across her face.

51

"Stay outta my fucking business! The only reason yo trick ass here was cuzza her… and hell yeah I'm looking, cuz Im'ma fuck Jaz like I ain't never fuck you. The fuck you thought trick ass bitch!" He snapped, searching around for his lighter. The blunt hung from his lips. Max's soul was hurting.

"Jaz don't want any uneducated ass nigga like you… Fuck You! That's why I'm fucking one of yo boys anyway. You ain't got shit on him… wit yo coked up dick," she snapped back, before proceeding upstairs to pack her things. Dirk lit his blunt as he got lost in his thoughts.

Her words soon echoed, impeding the already fucked up thoughts that were in his head. Immediately he skipped two steps at a time getting upstairs. Dirk stood in the doorway of their bedroom inhaling hard on his blunt.

"Oh now you think you leaving too… Huh bitch?" Max ignored him. She only needed to make it to the elevator door and she was out. Grabbing the small suitcase she had just packed, she started towards the door. "Answer me!" Dirk demanded with hatred in his voice.

Choices and Consequences

"What Dirk… yea I'm leaving too, shit. You'd rather have her here anyway. She had been planning this shit forever. I should've left when she first asked me. She stayed cause of me... not you!" Max continued, as she strained to get past him.

Max sighed as she left the room. '*Halfway there*,' she thought to herself.

Almost immediately, she felt Dirk snatch her by the back of her hair. Blunt still burning; he forces her face down to the floor. He began kicking her. Max tried to fight through the pain. She wanted to scream but the kick to the stomach silenced her. He allowed her to stand. As she limped towards the stairs, he kicks her in the back. Max tumbled down the stairs feeling the sharp pain go through her ankle, as she felt her foot twist in between the steps. Her head hit the floor and blood gushed from the right corner near her temple.

Dazed she tried to get up but her ankle was severely broken. Dirk slowly walked down the stairs; blunt still blazing as he chokes. Max crawled to the elevator door. She didn't have the strength to lift herself up. Dirk inflicted one final blow, which left her unconscious, a right hook to the right side of her face. As she lay in a pool of blood, Dirk sat down to watch the Classy Freak video.

Chapter 6

Six years had passed. It was a dreary rainy day in Savanna Georgia. Jaz and Damon had relocated there in hopes that Dirk would never find them. Jaz continued her education until she graduated. Soon she was the proud owner and founder of Taylors Haven. Taylors Haven was a battered women's shelter that housed eight women. Mrs. Kim, a heavyset woman with silky white long hair, was Jaz's manager. She was also the first tenant to live in Taylors Haven. Just looking at her face revealed the harsh life she had survived.

Mrs. Kim was a beautiful person inside and had become a great friend to Jaz. She knew just as much as Jaz when it came to the shelter and more when it came to the streets. Jaz welcomed her assistance, knowing she could learn a lot from her.

Jerry was the handyman for Taylors Haven and had a crush on Mrs. Kim. Yet, he never said anything.

Damon was the owner of a record shop for vintage LP's and novelties from back in the day. Ironically, the shop was called Back N Da Day Memorabilia. Even though the years had passed, Jaz often thought about Nana and Max but was still pleased at the life she had been blessed with thus far. She tried reaching her Nana by phone and mail but nothing came of it. The number had been disconnected and her mail was returned unopened. Jaz had it all, a man who loved her, a beautiful home and she was living her dream of helping people, especially women. There was only one thing missing… a baby.

For 2 years now, they had been trying to conceive. A few times, she thought she was pregnant but it turned out to be false alarms. When she got discouraged, Damon would always say that he loved practicing and as long as they had each other, they were ok. Today, Jaz figured she'd talk to Mrs. Kim about what she was feeling. Mrs. Kim couldn't have children on the account of her ex-husband; who had beaten her when she was 5 months pregnant, which caused her to miscarry. Because of it, she had to have an emergency hysterectomy.

On Friday morning, in the kitchen of Taylors Haven, Jaz and Mrs. Kim were drinking coffee and discussing Jaz's concerns. Most of the women had already gone out, either searching for jobs, on interviews or schooling.

"You know what happened to me in the past so I won't go into that story," Jaz explains.

"And you don't have to. Hell, I know all about pain. I will say this though, God has a reason for everything he allows to happen and not happen. We may not always agree, or even understand his plan for us… but be sure of this… He knows." Mrs. Kim explained, as she sipped her coffee.

"I know… I know… I just don't understand," Jaz agrees.

"Well he understands… you just be patient." She adds.

"You right… I'll try." Jaz responded, with tears in her eyes feeling defeated.

"Look at your life and what you been through. Baby you have more than anyone I know at your age… what you all but 25, 26."

"Yea, 26…" Jaz responded with a smile.

"Okay and you are helping people baby. Be proud of yourself and know that God will take care of you too," Mrs. Kim added, as she peered out the window from her chair.

"Mrs. Kim what you are you peeking at?" Jaz turned as she sips her coffee. Jaz got up and noticed a woman standing in the rain. '*Maybe she needed the assistance of Taylors Haven but was afraid to ask,*' Jaz thought to herself.

Mrs. Kim got up without a word and headed to the front door. "Ms.! Ms.! Do you need help?" Mrs. Kim called out to her. The woman didn't respond. By this time, Jaz had met Mrs. Kim at the door.

"You think she needs help?" Jaz whispered, "Well, if she does then she needs to say something. "You know I don't trust anybody." Jaz unlocked the bars on the screen door. Mrs. Kim reaches for her arm.

"Be careful now, Ms. Jaz," she told her. Jaz nodded and went out to the woman with an umbrella.

"Excuse me… do you need help?" The woman slowly turned. Her face looked oddly familiar. Life had dealt her a bad hand and it showed. Jaz's heart went out to the woman.

"Jaz it's me… Max." she spoke softly, her voice almost traumatized.

"Max?" Jaz looked puzzled. As her eyes watered with tears, she drops the umbrella and hugs Max as tight as she could. Max hugs her just as tight as she began to cry. "It's okay Max, everything will be okay. I got you." Max knees almost buckled. "Come on, let's get out this rain girl." Jaz added.

Mrs. Kim had walked back to her chair after opening the door for the two of them. Jaz took Max's coat and had her remove her soaked shoes, while giving her some house shoes that were by the door.

"Come on in here and have a seat. Let me get you something hot to drink."

"Coffee would hit the spot Jaz… thanks." Max sat down across from Mrs. Kim, who kept a close eye on her. She knew all about Max and what happened back in Detroit. Jaz soon sat too.

"Mrs. Kim this is Max. Max this is Mrs. Kim." she introduced the two.

"Well, Ms. Jaz I'm going out to the grocery store. Be back shortly, Max." Mrs. Kim said, as she gave Max the nod. Jaz could feel the tension but ignored it.

"Okay, you be careful. It's a mess out there." Jaz added, as she sips her coffee. Max sipped her coffee and waited for Mrs. Kim to leave.

"So what's been going on? How did you end up here?" Jaz inquired. Max cleared her throat.

"Well, I left Dirk after he broke my jaw and a couple of ribs."

"Oh my God Max!" Jaz almost cried out as she covers her mouth.

"I'm okay now Jaz. You are so sensitive." Max tried to laugh it off.

"Well, it didn't really end there. He came to see me when I was in the hospital and said if I told anybody he was gon kill me. The day I was released, he showed up to pick me up. By then I was too scared not to go home wit him." Max explained.

Choices and Consequences

"Max." Jaz whispered as tears form in her eyes.

"Things seemed to be okay for a couple of months. I ended up pregnant but he beat me wit a pistol cuz he said I tried to trap him." Max cried out. Jaz broke down as well.

"I lost my baby Jaz." Max continued to cry.

"Max I'm so sorry." Jaz got up and hugged Max. Max began to apologize for everything she said, done and didn't do.

After about an hour, they ended up in the living room. The crying had stopped as they talked. Jaz explained how Taylors Haven came to be. Before long, Mrs. Kim came back and put the groceries away. She entered into the living room.

"So Ms. Max, are you staying with us?" Max looked at Jaz. She didn't want to stay there. It was nice and all but she knew Jaz didn't live there. "Don't worry, you'll be safe here." Mrs. Kim added. Jaz knew how Max was and felt that Max didn't want to stay either.

"Well Mrs. Kim, I think Max will be coming to stay with me and Damon," Jaz replied. That didn't sit well with Mrs. Kim because she didn't trust Max.

"Well if you say so Ms. Jaz." Mrs. Kim responded, as she turned and went into the kitchen.

"Where's your bathroom Jaz?" Max asks.

"Down the hall and to the left…" Jaz replied. Mrs. Kim waited till Max closed the bathroom door; she walked back into the living room. "Are you sure about this Ms. Jaz?" Mrs. Kim questioned her, as her hand rubbed her chin.

"I know how you feel about my safety Mrs. Kim but she left him and I have to help her… I feel like I owe her that much." Jaz responded. Mrs. Kim shook her head.

"You don't owe anybody a thang except God… I hope you know what you're doing Ms. Jaz; I really do." she said, with her hand placed over her heart. Jaz got up and hugged Mrs. Kim. "I love you like a mother Mrs. Kim; you know that." Jaz laughed, as Mrs. Kim tooted her lips into a half smile, while returning a big hug.

"Yet… you listen to me as much as my own child would… not enough… but I love you too! Just please be careful. I got an ugly feeling about that

Max." she stated. Jaz smiled and shushed Mrs. Kim as she walked to meet Max, who was now standing over at the fireplace in the living room. "Tell you what; you take a vacation. How about a month away from this place? You and your friend get reacquainted."

"A month... Mrs. Kim are you sure?" "What, you don't think I can run this place by my lil old lonesome? Besides, I got Jerry." she smiled, her hand on her hip.

"Oh, I know you can handle this place and Mr. Jerry for that matter." Jaz laughs, as she hits the keypad to unlock her truck. Max was looking over the pictures on the fireplace mantle.

"Those are all the ladies who have come through these doors. Some came back to let us know how they were doing and well... some didn't." Mrs. Kim told Max, as she too entered the living room.

Max nodded. "Whew, this one right here look like a butch... who was she running from... a woman?" Max laughed.

"Well... she was a woman who preferred women and no she wasn't running from another woman. If you must know, her name is Tamika. We don't use labels in this house. Now I don't know where you-."

"No, we don't use labels Max." Jaz interrupted nicely, hurrying Max to the screen door.

"I'm sorry, but can we cut this short. I have to unlock my truck and everything now." Jaz laughs. She knew Mrs. Kim was about to lay into Max.

"Alright now." Mrs. Kim said, shaking her head.

"Well, guess I'll see you in a month. Keep me updated; will you?" Mrs. Kim told Jaz as she headed for the kitchen. She couldn't stand any more of Ms. Max.

"I sure will and get you some rest too." Jaz said, as she gently pulled Max's arm and headed out the door to her 2000 Red Grand Cherokee. It made her smile every time she looked at it.

As Jaz drove away, Mrs. Kim frowned. "Lord, be with her," she said, as she locked up.

They drove to Kudzu Café to pick up some lunch to take home. Kudzu had the best-smoked pork chops in town as far as Jaz was concerned.

"How is Damon gonna feel about me being there? Maybe I shouldn't stay." Max said.

"Well he's out of town on business won't be back for 2 weeks... so it's just us and anyway I'll tell him. It'll be okay. You'll see." Jaz told her, as she continued to drive. Max said nothing. She just frowned her eyebrows, as if to say yeah okay.

Chapter 7

Over the next few weeks, Jaz and Max did some of everything. They shopped over at Buck head, which had the hottest boutiques and upscale salons; they got manicures pedicures, new hair do's, clothes and shoes. With Dirk they could do all of the same things but for some reason it was more rewarding this time. Soon they pulled up to Jaz and Damon's home. It was an almond; with white trim, four-bedroom. It was an amazing mini mansion, with a beautiful landscape lawn. It was complete with Greek statues on each side of the driveway.

"Wow! Jaz, now this is living girl!" Max said, as she exited the truck. Jaz smiled at Max.

"Well, my home is yours till you can get on your feet." Jaz said, as she grabbed most of the bags from the backseat.

Max followed, as she almost forgot she even had bags. That night Jaz found Max crying in the living room. "Max… what's wrong?"

"Jaz, I am so sorry for everything; I mean it! I just want things the way they were." she sobbed.

"Hey, we already had this talk right and I'm sorry for leaving you back there. Max, things can't be the way they were you know… But they can be better right?" Jaz added, as she smiled holding Max.

"Yeah, I guess; but I promise you Jaz that I am going to get a job get on my feet and…"

"I know, I know and I'm here to help you anyway I can… okay?" "Thank you Jaz! Thank you so much!" Max added, as she leaned over and hugged Jaz.

The next day Jaz and Max went site seeing. Max put in a few applications for jobs and checked out the colleges. Damon called while they were out. Max overheard Jaz almost pleading with Damon to let her stay. Finally, it sounded like he agreed but only for Jaz's sake. He informed Jaz that his trip was cut short and he'd be home tomorrow. Afterward, the two continued their day visiting the sites and shopping at the grocery store.

They ended the day back at Jaz's place to cook some dinner. They laughed and talked. Jaz asked Max how she knew where to find her. Max told her that she assumed since Damon came from Atlanta, that is probably where they would end up. Max went on to say that a woman at the bus station asked if she needed a place to stay. She probably guessed that she was running from someone by her battered face. Max continued to explain that the woman had mentioned a woman's shelter owned by a woman Jasmine Taylor, and that's when she knew it had to be her.

Jaz couldn't tell if Max was lying or not so, she shook it off. They ate and watched movies till Jaz called it a night and went to bed.

The next morning Damon slips into the room quietly, putting his luggage down and completely undressing, he climbed into bed and nestled against Jaz.

"I love you," he whispers in her ear.

"I love you more!" she replied, as she smiled, while turning towards him to give him a kiss. She could feel his hardness poking at her. They explored each other's mouth with lust. Their hands were touching every part of each other. Damon always made it a point to please her body in every way imaginable. This time Jaz wanted to do something for him. Jaz sat up in the bed removing her gown. Her nipples were swollen. Damon reaches up to taunt each one. She positions Damon so that he was spread eagle before her. As she strokes his hardness, he gasps. Soon he watched in awe as Jaz bent down, with her wet tongue caressing his hardness before consuming him inside her warm mouth. He cried out her name. She smiles, as her mouth pleases him.

Unknowingly to both of them, Max was watching from the door that was ajar just enough for them not to see her. But, it was ajar just enough for her to see them. Jaz got up and climbed on top of Damon; her soft body rolling back and forth as she felt Damon deeper and deeper inside her. They both let out inaudible moans as he pulled her toward him kissing her breasts. Damon couldn't take it anymore. He sat up and rolled Jaz over. Now she was under him. He inserted slowly into her, making sure she felt every inch of him, as she squeezed his muscular arms.

"Baby," she moaned quietly.

"Yeah... I missed you too." he smiled, as he pushes deeper and harder.

He soon placed one of her legs over his shoulder and he went even deeper. Max stood watching and touching herself. She wanted to feel Damon. She wanted to feel that soft caressing love. Max placed her fingers inside of her; pushing hard against her g spot. Her eyes closed as she came hard on her hand. That was enough; Max couldn't stand there any longer, as her own juices flowed down her legs, she immediately went back to her room. She listened as Damon continued to make passionate love to Jaz.

The next morning Damon got up, showered and dressed. He then made Jaz's favorite breakfast, which was bacon, cheese eggs and buttermilk pancakes; topped with strawberries.

Anything strawberry was Jaz's favorite; her bath gel, hair mist and body mist. Damon smiled as he placed strawberries on top of the pancakes. He began thinking of her strawberry everything and thinking about last night. The phone rang, jarring him from his thoughts; as did the hot bacon grease popping on his arm. Quickly, he took the bacon out and turned the stove off. Wiping his hands on the kitchen towel, he hurried to the phone.

"Hello."

"Hey, what's up wit the shipment?"

"What! I told you not to discuss business on these land lines and cells for that matter nigga; and why the fuck you calling me at home and not on my cell?" Damon said, getting frustrated.

"Sorry D… just that, uh, yo mans didn't show up down at the shop that's all."

"Yeah alright... I'll take care of it… and don't fucking call me at home!" Damon almost yelled as he slammed the phone down.

Damon stood and his hands were rubbing the top of his head before searching his pockets for his cell to make a call.

"Hello… Carlos, what the fuck man! I sent my man's down and u didn't show!"

"Yeah, well I only deal with you D, no one else. I don't trust people and you know that I don't know them fucks!" a Cuban voice replied.

"Yeah, well I had other shit to tend to C; now you wanta make money or not? If you do, meet me at my place in the next hour… and C don't waste my time!" he added, as he slaps his cell closed. Max stood on the stairs listening the whole time. She looked back upstairs thinking if she would let Jaz know or not. But no, she had a better plan. Max came downstairs. "Good morning, something smells good." Damon looked at her as he approached the kitchen. He was wondering if she heard anything.

"Good morning Max. Is Jaz up yet?"

"Naw, she is sleeping like a baby."

"Okay, well let her know I'll call her. I got some errands to run."

"Will do." she nodded, as she took a bite of the bacon he had prepared for her and Jaz.

Moments later Jaz came down all sleepy eyed "Hum mm… Something smells good… Where's Damon?" she stopped to look around.

"Oh... he said he will call you later; he has some errands to run." Max delivers the message, as she got up to rake out her half eaten breakfast.

"Jaz… can I use your truck for a while. I wanta ride around and put in some more apps."

"Yeah… Do you want me to go with you?"

"Naw girl, just relax. I'm good." Max replied, as she headed upstairs to shower. After about 20 minutes, Max came down. "Alright Lady... I'm out."

"Bye," Jaz said, with her hand up in the air dangling the keys to her truck.

"Thank you." Max grabs for the keys and rushes out the door. Immediately, she began inputting Damon's record shop into the GPS. Driving a short distance down the street from the shop she parked and watched. She noticed two foreigners standing outside talking to Damon. They laughed, and then went in through the back way. She quickly got out and hurried down the street; careful not to be noticed. She knew it wouldn't be wise to go in through the front, so she walks around looking for a way in. She found a door that was locked.

Max being Max didn't care about getting dirty; as she looked down to see a window which was half way opened. Looking around, she pried it open just enough for her to crawl through.

While creeping up the back stairs and peering around the corner, she saw Damon, another guy and the two foreigners who were outside. "*Hell naw!*" she whispered to herself. Damon was still in the game, she thought to herself, as she watches Damon's guy test the coke from that was in a briefcase on the table. Once it turned blue, the men exchange the money. Max shook her head *'this is gonna hurt Jaz she seriously thought this fool had a real job.'* She thought to herself.

Soon after, Max hurried to the car. Sitting, she continued to watch from the rear view and side mirrors as she hunched down in the seat. Shortly, the men, along with Damon and his guy came out and gave each other dap, before they proceeded to leave. Damon pulled off alone. She tried following; him staying at least two cars behind him. Unfortunately, she lost him in traffic.

Chapter 8

Max drove around a few more blocks while searching for his truck. Then there he was. It looked like he was driving out of town somewhere. '*This must be the worst part of Georgia*,' she thought to herself; as he pulled up to what looked like an abandoned street. No houses were occupied, accept one that no one should be living in.

With them being the only vehicles on the block she knew she couldn't sit anywhere. Suddenly, he waved his hand at her to drive to him.

Her heart raced a mile a minute. She wondered if he knew she was following him but was unsure. So, she drove down to where he was while attempting to calm herself. She pulled up on the side of Damon, who was now leaning on his truck.

"I know, I know, I'm fucking lost... duh!" Max tried to laugh her nervousness off.

"Yea, you are but it's cool. A lot of people get lost who isn't from here... shit I got lost when I moved here the first time so where you headed?" Damon asks, trying not to let her know he saw her following him.

"Shit, I was going to put in some apps and do a little site-seeing but I also need to holler at you on the real. I didn't want to talk at the house." she added. Damon's jaws clenched

"Well park and come ride with me. I got some stuff I gotta do and we can talk on the way." he explains.

Max nodded as she pulled in front of his truck and parked. Max smiled as she walked to his truck but Damon was boiling on the inside as he climbed in.

"So let's talk Max." Damon drove to what seemed like even a more seedy side of town. Max went on to explain to him that she fantasizes about him and on more than one occasion and she wanted him, just once in real life. Damon was quiet for a few moments, till he laughed, which pissed Max off.

"Are you fucking crazy!" he laughs. Max's face turns angry.

"Tell you what; if you don't give me what I want I guess I'll just have to tell Jaz that you're still in the game. And yes, I do have proof. Yeah, I saw everything today. You really should get that basement window fixed." Max laughs.

Damon knew what she was talking about. *'How did she know about the window being broken if she wasn't there?'* He thought to himself. He needed to think of something quick. "Well... what we doing Damon?" Max stared with her arms folded.

"I guess you got me this time but Max this is a onetime deal and I don't want to hear about this shit later?" Damon agreed.

"That's what's up, that's all I ask," she added, with a devilish smile.

Damon pulls off and drives what seems to be two blocks away from where they were and it was still a fucked up neighborhood. "Where the hell are we? I know don't nobody live here... unless this is one of your spots," she questioned.

"Exactly… Come on. I gotta take care of some business right quick." he added, as they enter the shack of a house.

"Damn D, who dis?" one of the guys ask, who was in the living room playing a video game.

"My girl, Max… Max give me minute," he said, almost through his teeth, as if it hurt to even say her name. Damon walks to the bathroom and closes the door.

"Hello everybody." she spoke, as she waved to the two guys in the living room and the hood rat chick at the kitchen table playing cards wit herself. She looks like the chick from the picture.

"Have a seat ma… oh my name Smoke… you got a man?"

"Ah yeah, didn't you hear him introduce me?" she proclaimed with attitude. Everybody laughs were followed by a hell naw. Damon returns and motions for Max to follow him she did. They went down to the basement. It looked like a club, complete with poles lights and bar. "This is cool as hell D."

"Thanks come in here." Max followed him into a room where the walls were painted a blood red. The floor was painted black; the only light in the room was a black light, which only gave shadows of them. It was a decked out fucking room basically.

"So I guess this the place where my fantasies come true huh?" Max laughed, with excitement as she began snapping her fingers.

"Ah yeah," Damon said, twisting his mouth. He knew this was some straight bullshit. He looked over at Max, who was sitting on the bed and unbuttoning her shirt; soon to be releasing her large breast. Damon couldn't help but feel the swelling in his jeans. Even the black light couldn't hide them big kitties. He walked over and stood in front of her. Saying nothing, she grabbed his hardness and proceeded to lick the head. Her mouth soon slid up and down, faster and faster. Damon was turned on as he taunted her breast, which made Max get even more into what she was doing.

Damon quickly felt himself about to cum and he pushed Max's head up off him. He wouldn't give her the satisfaction of making him cum.

"You ready for this?" he forces a smile, while gripping his hard dick in his hand.

"Hell yeah baby!" Max replied, as she stood to get completely undress.

Damon's phone vibrated. He quickly fixed his jeans and headed for the door.

"Where you going?"

"Give me one second Max," he said, looking at his phone.

"Well turn on a light or something. You can't see shit in this muthafucka." she laughs.

"Ain't no light for this room Max. Just hold on; relax I got you." he told her as he exited the room.

Max rolled over onto her stomach, relaxing her head across her arms. She closed her eyes and smiled at the thought of feeling Damon inside her. Soon the door opens and closes. Hands squeeze her ass, as fingers almost immediately tantalize her clit from the back. As it began to swell, the fingers fucked her insides. She fucked back harder and harder as she came with a gush. "Damn!" the low voice muttered. Suddenly, the door opens again. Now a light from another part of the basement was on.

Max turned around fast, she was feeling like some bullshit was going on.

"What the fuck! Where is Damon!" she screams, as she scrambles to get up and grab her clothes.

"Damn! Mika," a male voice yells. "Nigga fuck dat. You down here trying make love to the bitch like we ain't waitin' and shit!" Mika screams back.

Max continued to ask where Damon was. "He ain't here ma." another man's voice responded. His was deeper almost scary. Standing in the door way he stood at least 300lbs. He was solid at 6'3, with a fro.

"Who the fuck are you? "Where the fuck is Damon!" she screamed again, as she continued to call his name, as if he were somewhere in the house.

Suddenly the big man slaps Max so hard that she has a blackout. "Bitch! I told you he ain't here!" he griped.

"Come on Moe; it ain't that fuckin serious man!" Smoke shouted, as he began to feel things were going too far. Moe was intimidating in character and had a rep for being cold-hearted.

83

Damon didn't too much care for him but kept him around for the shit that needed to be done by someone with no conscience.

Moe stood staring at Max's naked body. He looks at Mika and Smoke and smiles as he walks toward Max's limp body.

"Ya'll can watch or get the fuck out." he griped again.

"This some bullshit…" Smoke said as he and Mika headed back upstairs.

Moe threw Max on the bed; squeezing and sucking hard on her breasts. After groping every part of her he forced his "hung" like a horse dick inside her deeper and deeper, as he pushed himself inside. Max began to wake up due to the pain. She screamed trying to push him off her. But her strength was no match to this big man. Every time she tried to push or tried to get up he punched her in the face till her eyes were swollen shut. She was now motionless.

Mika and Smoke sat in the kitchen listening to Moe grunt and talk shit to Max. This went on for about 2 hours. Moe had fucked every hole Max had. He was brutal to say the least.

"I'm done with that bitch now; it's on ya'll," Moe said, as he came up the stairs adjusting his pants.

"I'm straight," Mika said, as she looked down at the table trying not to look at Moe.

"Yea, I'm good too." Smoke added. They didn't want any part of it anymore.

"Shit, I guess I'll take both ya'll turn then. Shit! It ain't nothing to a G!" he laughed, as he proceeded back downstairs.

Moe went into the room and noticed that Max was no longer on the bed. Walking around to the other side he saw her lying on the floor. Moe snatched Max up off the floor and threw her onto the bed.

"Bitch, where you thought you were going, huh?" he cursed her.

All Max could do was release a painful moan. Her body was limp and her face felt like it was falling apart. Abruptly, Moe forces his hardness into her asshole once again. Max couldn't even scream as excruciating pain shot through her whole body.

Moe rode her ass as if he were riding a horse; wrapping her long hair around his fist. He pulled it back with each thrust. Once he came, he got up and tried to put his nasty dick in her mouth and she bit down as hard as she could. Moe bellowed out the loudest scream imaginable. He began punching Max in the head as hard as he could, until she let go. He slowly got up and grabbed his 9, placing a pillow over her head. He fired one shot.

"Stupid Bitch!" he shouted, as he got his self together and exited the room. Smoke and Mika ran downstairs, running into Moe.

"What the fuck man!" Smoke shouted.

"Dat bitch bit my shit... fuck dat bitch. I bet cha she won't be biting any more dicks now. I'm out this muthafucka!" Moe confirmed angrily.

Mika slowly walked in and took the pillow from Max's head. "Awe shit!" She jumped back as brain matter began falling onto the floor.

Chapter 9

Jaz woke up, as if she had a bad dream. She immediately got up, searched the house for Max, and looked out the window to see if her truck was back. But, no Max or truck and it was 4:15 a.m.

"Baby… Baby!" She awakened Damon, as his eyes squint, trying to open them enough to focus on her.

"Baby what's wrong?" his grumbling voice answered.

"Damon, it's 4 in the morning and Max is not here. Something happened; what if Dirk… Baby just go look for her please!" Jaz pleaded.

Damon blew his breath. "Alright, alright damn! She's a grown ass woman baby. Maybe she wasn't ready to come home, shit!" he fussed, as he got up and searched the room for a pair of pants.

Jaz said nothing. Her silence let him know her feelings were hurt. Holding his jeans in his hand his head drooped toward the floor.

"I'm sorry baby. I'm just tired... but if it means that much to you I'll go look somewhere; hell everywhere... just get you some rest... okay!" he apologized.

"Thank you." she said, as she climbed slowly in the bed. He got dressed and left. As he sat in his truck his cell rung. The caller id showed Smoke and he knew something was wrong.

"Yeah Smoke..." he said with frustration in his voice.

"Man I don't know how to say this... but-"

"Smoke, just say it; damn!" Damon shouted.

"Man, yo man's Moe killed that chick Max. Shot her in the fucking head!" Smoke shouted, with nervousness in his voice.

"Fuck! I'm on my way, shit!" Damon belted out. This created an entire new set of problems he thought to himself, as his hands slid down his face.

When Damon got there and saw Max he felt bad. Moe had done a number on her; blood feces and brain matter was everywhere. He was trying to shake the sickness off that had settled in his stomach. He instructed Mika and Smoke to roll Max up in some plastic and clean the basement up with bleach. Damon went to get a large duffle bag and a sack of cement from the storage room. They kept shit like that around just for shit like this. Shortly, they placed Max inside the duffle bag and poured wet cement inside. Damon instructed Mika and Smoke to finish the job before morning. Once upstairs, Mika and Smoke told Damon what had happened while they smoked on a blunt. To them, that was like smoking a cigarette to calm their nerves.

"We gotta burn this bitch down, no evidence ya'll feel me... and don't leave the body in this house!" Damon commanded and they agreed. Damon left the house leaving Smoke and Mika to do as he instructed.

Arriving back at home the sun was now coming up and Jaz was asleep. Damon took a shower and climb into bed. Jaz felt him next to her as she nestled up to his chest.

"Baby did you find her?"

"No, but I'll look again today."

89

"Thank you. I'm worried." she mumbled, as she got comfortable.

"I know, that's why I'll keep looking." he replied, as he hugged her.

Over the next few days, her truck was found with no signs of foul play; only that it was stripped down. The fire at the spot wasn't reported. Maybe because it was a part of the neighborhood that people didn't care enough about. Jaz had filed a missing persons report for Max. She didn't really care about her truck. Ms. Kim had tried to talking to Jaz concerning the whereabouts of Max. But Jaz dismissed it. She already knew Ms. Kim had that I told you so look, so she knew what Ms. Kim was thinking. Damon had a new location and only Smoke knew about it. Mika was nowhere to be found nor was Moe. Jaz wondered if Max had headed back to Detroit.

Months went by and it was nearly Thanksgiving in a couple of weeks. Damon had been gone out of town for at least a couple of weeks now. Before he left he'd gotten Jaz a Burgundy CL 500. Back at Taylors Haven, life went on as usual. Mrs. Kim and a couple of the women were in the kitchen at Taylors Haven putting up Thanksgiving decorations and writing a grocery list for Thanksgiving dinner. Everyone knew about Jaz's Thanksgiving nightmare and tried to create new memories for her, especially around this time of year.

Jaz stood staring out the window. "Ms. Jaz, are you okay," Mrs. Kim asked.

Jaz sighed, "Feeling a little ill... but I'll be okay."

"Maybe you should go home and relax. I'll handle things here." Mrs. Kim responded.

"Yea, I think I will. Damon's plane lands this afternoon, so hopefully I'll be better by then."

"Okay, well I'll call and check on you later."

"Thanks Mrs. Kim." Jaz replied, as she grabs her keys and heads home.

As Jaz arrives home, she notices an old school gray Monte Carlo sitting in front of her house. She sat for a minute; her heart racing wondering if Dirk had finally found them. *Fuck it,* she thought to herself, as she exited her vehicle as if she was mad and ready to fuck somebody up. Jaz walks over to the vehicle and sees a woman. She wondered if maybe it was Max. Her eyes squint to get a better look as the woman who was slowly exiting the vehicle. "Tamika," she whispered to herself.

"Hey Ms. Jaz," Mika said, as she greeted her.

"Where have you been? Are you okay?" Jaz questioned, hugging Mika.

"Ms. Jaz, can we talk in private? I really need to talk to you."

"Okay, okay… what's wrong?" Jaz asks, as she led Mika up to the house.

"Where's Damon?" Mika asks, as she looks around.

"He's out of town at the moment so speak freely; it's okay." Soon after inside, Jaz extended her hand for Mika to have a seat. Mika began spilling her guts and crying telling everything she could concerning Damon, his business, Max and what had happen at the house. Of course, she was intentionally leaving out any detail of her involvement. She didn't realize that Max was a friend of Jaz's.

"Wait... wait… you mean to tell me that Damon had Max killed?"

"I'm really sorry Jaz.. I didn't realize you knew her. I would've come to you sooner." Mika cried.

Jaz sat down as she took in everything Mika had said, as tears fell from her eyes. Mika apologized repeatedly.

"I don't know what to do." Mika said, as she broke down once again. Jaz immediately felt nauseated and suddenly she jumped up and ran to the bathroom off the hallway. It was as if everything she ate that day came up and out as her brain tried to process everything Mika had told her. Jaz threw up, cried and threw up some more. Her heart was aching, as was her stomach and along came the onset of a migraine.

Her mind said Mika was lying because she hadn't seen this girl in over a year. But her gut fought against her telling her it was true. After about 20 minutes, she attempted to pull herself together washing her face and rinsing her mouth with water. Walking back toward the living room Jaz found her front door wide open and Mika speeding off.

Chapter 10

Days went by as she watched the news for any signs of what Mika had told her but there was none. She decided not to mention it to Damon until she knew for sure. Her mind struggled with the information she had received. How could her man, the love of her life, her future; know that her friend was dead? How could he lie about his job? So many thoughts ran threw her mind and she didn't know how to feel.

Taking a couple of Tylenol and a shower she laid down for a quick nap. Hours later Damon arrives home via taxi. Jaz had slept through his calls to pick him up. Damon stood in the doorway of their master bedroom staring at Jaz sleeping. '*She looked angelic*,' he thought to himself. Walking over to her, he gently sat on the bed and stroked her hair; opening her eyes halfway she saw his face and immediately jumps up clenching the covers to her chest in fear. Damon sat up. His face was puzzled and his hands flew up backing away. "Baby what's wrong... did something happen while I was gone cause you know I will fucking kill somebody if they hurt you!" he ranted, as he got up and paced around the room.

Jaz just stared at him as the words kill somebody ranged out. '*Did he let this happen to Max because of what happened in Detroit?*' she wondered. Damon walked over to the bed with tears in his eyes. "Baby, please tell me what's wrong... please Jaz." his eyes pleaded with her. As tears formed in her eyes, looking at him '*this was her man and she loved him with every piece of her soul. He couldn't have done what Mika said he did.*' Jaz thought.

Caressing Damon's face, "No one did anything to me... I just had a bad dream that's all... I love you so much Damon; so much more than you will ever know." she answered, as she gently kissed his soft lips. Damon moaned as his mouth explored hers.

"Jaz, I love you too. I'd do anything to keep you safe... you know that right?"

"Yes baby, I know." she smiled. Damon couldn't wait to get undressed as he slowly caressed Jaz's body through her pink see through nightgown; void of anything underneath. "You are so beautiful Jaz!" he added, as he gently bit her nipples through her gown. Jaz moaned; squeezing his body between her legs. She needed to feel him inside of her, despite everything she was told. She loved him and wouldn't let her mind think that he could do any of those things. Damon made love to Jaz in a way that convinced her that his heart couldn't do anything to hurt her.

Over the next couple of weeks it was life as usual although the thoughts of what Mika had told her ran cross her mind every now and then. She had convinced herself *'they were all lies because it would have been on the news, wouldn't it?'* she thought to herself.

She continued checking with the police department concerning her missing persons report for Max, but nothing came of it. It was a Saturday morning; Damon had left for the shop when Jaz got up and turned on the news by habit. She did her usual morning routine; showered and got dressed to head to Taylors Haven. She notices the pregnancy test box under the bed. Hoping Damon hadn't seen it yet she hurried over to the bed, grabs the box and heads for the master bathroom. Tearing open the box, she sat down and peed on the stick. She always felt like she was pregnant but they were always false alarms, so she wouldn't say anything to Damon unless she was sure.

Jaz had gotten into the habit of buying the test, just in case. Placing the stick on the back of the toilet, she finishes and proceeds to wash her hands.

Breaking News, the voice from the TV announces. Jaz stood at the sink awaiting the results of the test, as she listened closely to the breaking news. "22 year-old Tamika Jackson, known to friends as Mika, was found early this morning on Atlanta's eastside. Police say foul play was involved; more at 5." Jaz ran into the bedroom and watched in horror as they showed a picture of Mika and announced her murder. A sudden sadness came over her as she stood in their bedroom staring at the TV screen. She broke down and cried uncontrollably, as thoughts flooded her mind. She was losing everything! The man she loved was a liar, thief and killer. Her heart felt as if it were literally breaking. Feeling like she had just forgotten all about Max, she felt even worst.

Meanwhile, back in Detroit, Dirk had received a call from a guy who informed him that he had valuable information on Damon, Max and Jaz. But, the guy wanted money; 10 grand to be exact. Dirk agreed to pay. The guy said he would call him back with the meeting place for the exchange.

Back at Jaz's place, she packed a small suitcase and filled it with only a few items. *'The hell with the rest of that shit; I gotta get outta here.'* she thought to herself. Jaz drove and drove, until she found a motel as far away from home as possible. Once she checked in she sat down and called Mrs. Kim; informing her to keep watch over Taylors Haven. She expressed that she didn't know when or even if she'd be back. Changing the topic, Mrs. Kim started explaining what she saw on the news. Luckily, she didn't know anything except what the news reported. Mrs. Kim was unaware of any connection between Jaz and the story.

"Wow... did they say who killed her? I saw it earlier but they didn't say anything else. It's all really sad." Jaz stated, as she played having any knowledge of Mika's death off.

"Well, they just stated that they had no leads and that it looked like someone got away with cold blooded murder." Mrs. Kim replied.

Meanwhile, Damon had arrived home and found the master bedroom in shambles. Clothes were thrown everywhere and it looked as if someone was looking for something. He immediately got scared and angry. *'Something must have happened... Did Dirk find us and take Jaz?'* he thought, as he went through the house calling out for her. Running back upstairs and looking over the bedroom once more, he then turned to the bathroom door that was closed. "Jaz..." He almost cried, fearing the worst, as he stormed into the bathroom. But, there was no Jaz. There was only the pregnancy test that was left on the back of toilet. She'd forgotten to grab it.

Damon picked up the test and saw the two lines. Jaz was pregnant. Hurrying to his truck he then drove to Taylors Haven to speak with Mrs. Kim. He hoped that Jaz was there. Mrs. Kim wouldn't even open the security bars for Damon.

Speaking with him through the security bars was as close as he would get. Mrs. Kim finally convinced him that she knew nothing. Damon stood in front of Taylors Haven and called Smoke. "What up boss man... you back?" Smoke answered.

"Yeah, yeah... look Jaz is missing. My fucking house is ransacked and I know that fool Dirk got her. I don't know how or when, but I'm a kill that nigga!" he began to shout.

"Shit, he musta' got Mika too; that shit all on the news man!"

"What!" Damon yelled.

"Yeah man... they found Mika dead this morning. I don't know what da fuck is going on!" Smoke replied. In frustration,

Damon wiped his face with his free hand. "Fuck! Look, let me hit you back!" Damon shouted in frustration.

"Yep..." Smoke replied calmly, as he hung up.

Damon got in his truck. As he tried to figure things out, soon he was punching the steering wheel. "What the fuck man!" he yelled.

Back at the motel it seemed to get later and later. Jaz had contacted the Savannah PD. She was scared, hurt and feeling alone because her life was falling apart before her eyes. Detective Jason Keyes had spoken with Jaz concerning the investigation and the information she had. He assured her that she would be safe and asked that she'd come into the station soon as possible. Shaken, she grabs her purse and headed to the door. Suddenly there was a knock at the door and it startled her.

"Yes…" her voice quiet.

"Housekeeping…" a woman's voice replied. Jaz released a deep sigh of relief as she opened the door. A small woman stood before her with clean white towels in hand.

"Thank you." Jaz smiled.

"Good evening mamma." the woman replied, as she nodded and walked away.

Jaz placed the towels on the bed and turns back to head out.

Suddenly Damon was standing in the open doorway. She didn't know whether to scream or cry. "Damon…" her voice whispered in a quiet and nervous tone. Damon slowly entered as he closed and locked the door. As he turned around he faced Jaz with his hands up, as if he were in a hold up. He saw the fear in her face.

"Jaz, please let me explain." he pleaded with a saddened tone.

Jaz broke down crying uncontrollably; her knees giving way from under her.

Damon immediately caught her. In spite of everything going on, his arms felt so good around her. His eyes were filled with tears of hurt. Damon picked Jaz up and carried her to the couch near the window. Easing her jacket off, as well as his... her heart wouldn't allow her to stop him.

Damon got on his knees, attempting to explain that Max was an accident and that he wasn't even there when it happened. He just didn't know how he would explain that to her and that the only reason he was still in the game was due to him owing some people a lot of money. He was sorry that he had lied. Jaz's heart wanted to believe him but her mind said, '*Get your ass outta there.*' As we know, we as women tend to go with our hearts instead. Damon caresses her stomach while looking up at her with heartfelt tears.

"Baby you are my life and you carrying a part of both of us which is our family. That's all I need," he cried, with his head on her lap.

Jaz began to cry too as she rubbed his head. *'Family... the pregnancy test musta been positive,'* she figured. Damon rises up and hugged Jaz's waist.

"I need you Jaz." He continued to cry.

Tears rolled down her face as she hugged his head tight. Her mind was in a continuous battle with her heart. Soon, Damon lifts her blouse over her stomach and begins kissing her stomach. Smoothly, he begins to unbutton her blouse. "Damon..." she moans softly.

"Baby, I love you with everything in me..." he replied, as he unfastens her bra from the front. Releasing her swollen breasts, passionately he tongue kisses each one. His hands journey downward, unhooking her jeans, while his mouth pleasured her erect nipples. Her back arches as her breasts rise to meet him. Damon stopped and stared at her long enough to see her eyes close and open again.

"I love you!" he spoke. Jaz reached for his face; her hands slowly caressing it. She'd almost forgotten how good his skin felt. Love just seemed to pour out of each of them with each touch.

Damon soon removed her boots, while sliding her jeans and pink lace panties off in one motion. He was gently massaging her body, starting at her feet, as he reached her thighs. He parted her legs as his hands began massaging upward to her swollen clit. She opened her legs even farther.

Lowering his head and leaning back on her arms, she soon felt the tip of his tongue slide between her wetness. Jaz gasps as her body begins to squirm. Damon made love to her body with his mouth, before completing his task. Damon's hardness was pulsating to the point of an ache. He quickly got undressed. His hands appreciated every curve and dipped along her body. Even her imperfections were perfect to him.

His lips and tongue did a job on her swollenness, as she began to shudder. He knew this meant she was about to cum. His tongue kissed passionately at her warm liquids. Jaz almost screamed. Damon rose up and Jaz scooted to the headboard.

Slowly, he inserted his hardness inside of her. She was more than moist at this point. "Oh my goodness," he moaned at the slickness. Jaz seemed to pull him deeper inside of her; as her kegel exercises always came in handy. His pace quickened as he went deeper. They were so close that they could feel each other's heart racing. Jaz's mind wouldn't allow her to think. Damon could feel each time she came and it was an overflow. It gushed against the head of his hardness. Damon withheld his time to explode. Once he knew, now was the time to pull out and he did. "Damon no... please!" she whimpered, but Damon felt the need to give her every pleasure imaginable. As his head soon disappeared once again between her legs, Jaz closes her eyes as she felt his tongue penetrate her. She bit her bottom lip, as Damon's tongue skillfully made love to her again. Soon her legs began to tremble and tighten. He knew she was ready once more.

His tongue went into frenzy, as it darted in and out of her, while tasting her warm juices. Damon came up and reinserted himself. Slowly, her legs wrapped around his waist. His strokes became longer and deeper, pulling out to the head, only to plunge deeper again. This drove her crazy as she called out his name. A powerful gush hit the head of his dick once again. He soon felt an intense sensation of drunkenness. He couldn't hang on any longer. He exploded just as she was again too. They felt stunned by the passion that had engulfed both of them.

Soon after collapsing onto her body, Damon remembered that she was pregnant. He then hurried to roll on the side of her. Jaz smiled because she knew why he hurried onto her side. They both lay silently. Soon, they drifted off to sleep; not thinking of anything only feeling.

Chapter 11

The next morning Jaz quietly showered and got dressed carefully; not to wake Damon. She grabbed the few things that she had brought with her and then she paused and stared at Damon, who was sound asleep. He looked so peaceful. Feeling as if her soul ached with pain, she *'wondered how many storms this life would throw at her.'* Tears filled her eyes, as her mind reminisces from how they met to now. She wishes that this was a nightmare that she'd soon wake from but it wasn't. She knew what needed to be done. Jaz gently rubbed her stomach as she headed out the door for check out.

Heading to the police station she was stopped at a red light. Her thoughts began to consume her once again. *'Here you are getting ready to put your child's father in jail. You may not ever see him again and this baby will never know his or her father. Damon would have been a great dad. Where's your loyalty? You say you love him; you already know he loves you.'* Jaz felt as if she was doing Damon wrong. She was supposed to have his back no matter what. Max was loyal in her relationship with Dirk. *'You need to make this right for Max.'* her thoughts continued. Suddenly, a car honked from behind; jarring her to pay attention to the now green light. Jaz began driving again. Moments later she pulled into the police station parking lot. Sitting in her car she checked her face in the overhead mirror, as she attempted to get herself together.

Upon opening car door her cell rang. It was Damon but she didn't answer. He eventually left a voicemail after calling back at least three more times. Jaz inhaled and exhaled before heading for the front door of the station. Suddenly, her cell sings a song and she knew that it was a text. Stopping, she read it. *'I love you no matter what.'* The text from Damon read. Jaz sighed, as she continued through the doors of the station while never replying to Damon's text or calls.

Once inside she arrived at the desk. "Detective Keyes, please. My name is Jasmine Taylor. He's expecting me."

"Oh Yes, Ms. Taylor come this way." a woman officer said, as she motions for Jaz to follow her. "Detective Keyes… Jasmine Taylor is here to see you."

"Thanks Jones," he replies. "Ms. Taylor, please have a seat." he said, as he got up to close the door behind the woman officer.

"Thank you." Jaz replied, as she began to cry. He handed her a napkin.

"I know this is very difficult for you. I can't begin to imagine any words of comfort I could offer to you… and please call me Jason." he added, as he sat down behind his desk.

They talked for at least two hours. He tried not to stare at this beautiful woman in front of him. Her heart held so much love and pain. He wanted to save her and help her to smile again. However, she probably thought of him as the bad guy. After all, he's the one who is leading the investigation. He couldn't understand what drew him to her so much. He didn't even know her.

Meanwhile, Dirk had arrived in Savanna, along with Cash to meet up with the guy who called him. The guy said he'd be wearing a black hat with the letter M on it; outlined in white and a red and black falcons coat in the front of Kudzu Café. "Hey, that's that nigga right there D." Cash almost shouted, as he pointed to the guy. Dirk looks up and there he was; the nigga who was trying to gank him out this cash. Dirk rolled down the back window and whistle to the guy.

"Hey, are you looking for Dirk?"

"Yeah, yeah... that's you?"

"Yep, hop in dog?" Dirk added, as he slid over to the other side of the back seat.

They drove off riding around talking. The guy introduces himself as Moe. He told Dirk where Jaz and Damon lived and what happened to Max. Only, he put it all on Damon. After Dirk put ten grand in his hand they parked at a nearby park and Dirk told him that their business was done. When Moe attempted to get out, Cash turned around with a 45 in his face. He began pleading for his life and he even offered to give the money back. While he was concentrating on Cash, Dirk pulled a small pillow from the floor and shot Moe in the side of the head with a 9 millimeter. It had a silencer attached to the front of it.

Cash laughed! "That nigga didn't know what was coming huh, huh!" he shouted all hyped up, like he got high off the whole ordeal.

"Naw; country ass nigga didn't know who he was fucking wit. Gemme my damn money, fool!" Dirk frowned as he snatched the money from Moe's dead hand.

"You outta here; you country ass nigga!" Dirk stated, as he opened the door and kicked Moe's body out.

"Alright, let's head to Damon's place. We gon' finish dis shit to-day." Dirk added, as he lit a blunt.

Moments later, Dirk and Cash sat down the street from Jaz and Damon's house. They were far enough to see the house and far enough to go unnoticed, as they sniffed powder and bullshitted about what they were going to do. Detective Keyes escorted Jaz to her car. He reassured her that he would be by after his shift to check on her. She agreed and headed home although Keyes told her to stay away from her house until contacted. Jaz was tired. *'It had been a long ass day,'* she thought to herself. All she wanted to do was take a warm bath and sleep. She didn't know if Damon would come home or not. *'If he did, how would the night proceed?'* she wondered. Jaz looked at her watch as she opened the front door. *'It is already dark and barely nine thirty.'* she thought, as she punched in the code to turn the alarm off.

Suddenly, she realizes that she had left her phone in the car. As she opened the door, she was shocked to see Dirk and Cash, as they forced their way in.

Chapter 12

Meanwhile, Detective Keyes received a call about a dead body being found in a nearby park. He instantly thought of Damon, so he made a call to Jaz. There was no answer. He felt something was wrong and that somehow this was all connected. He immediately got in his car and headed for her place.

"Don't let anyone contaminate my fucking crime scene. I'll be there shortly… I gotta check on something and I'm pretty damn sure it's related to our dead body." Detective Keyes commanded, before hanging up.

Before Jaz could scream, Cash placed his hush finger to his lips. It was his way of letting her know not to even think about it. They forced their way in and closed the door.

"Surprised to see me?" Dirk asks, with a crazed look in his eyes.

"More appalled than anything." She replied, with repulsion.

Dirk smiled and Cash gave her a right hook that sent her straight to the floor. She already knew not to fight, let alone scream. Cash was a grimy ass nigga who cared very little for human life. He would have shot her with no doubt.

Dirk grabbed Cash's arm. "That's enough; I don't want'a fuck dat pretty face unless..." he ended his sentence.

Cash dragged her upstairs to what he assumed to be the master bedroom, and he was right. Pulling a chair out of the corner, he forces Jaz to sit.

Dirk came up with his gun in hand. "I'll keep an eye on this bitch... you go downstairs and find some tape. Check the kitchen; shit check everywhere. I know they got some tape in this big mutha fucka." Dirk told Cash.

Cash ran thru the house scouring for tape in every room until he found some in the basement closet.

Cash came back to the bedroom with a roll of duct tape. He immediately started taping Jaz to the chair as she cried. Dirk grabbed a handful of her hair snatching her head back towards him.

"If you would have chosen me you wouldn't be in this predic-a-ment now would ya?" Dirk pronounced, as he bent down and kissed Jaz's bloody lip. "That's why you have to think… There are choices and there are consequences!" he stated, as he licked the blood from around his lips. Shoving her head forward he commanded, "Tape this bitch mouth shut!"

Cash's final strip stretched from ear to ear.

"Look for a safe. I know dat nigga Damon got some cash or sum'n in this bitch!" Dirk instructed, as he stood back and lit up a blunt.

Cash begin searching every room, from bottom to top; leaving no stone unturned. Outside, as Damon bends the corner, he notices Detroit plates on a truck similar to Dirks. Deciding to park a few houses down, Damon hopped out pistol in hand. He proceeded quietly up to the house. Hearing what appeared to be rambling coming from inside, he was sure it was Dirk.

Damon turned the knob at the front door, hoping the alarm wouldn't sound. It didn't. He saw

Cash in the study, which was adjacent to the stairs. Quietly, he moves along the wall till he reaches the study. He hears Dirks voice coming from upstairs "This how ya'll repay me... for all da shit I done for you and that bitch Max!" he shouts. "Yea and don't think I don't kno yo man had Max killed... Yea bitch I kno bout it... and don't think for a minute he gon get away wit it... nah, ain't' gon happen".

Jaz was scared now. She knew he was going to kill her to hurt Damon. Damon proceeded to creep up on Cash. He places his German Ruger to the back of Cash's head, at the same time disarming Cash of his weapon. Cash froze as if his life depended on it.

"Don't move..." Damon whispered. "Upstairs..." he commanded.

By this time, Detective Keyes had arrived outside. Spotting Jaz's car in the driveway he wondered why she didn't answer her phone. He approached the house soundlessly, as he peered through the windows for any movement. There was none, but he could hear talking from within the house. As he drew his weapon, he called for backup.

118

He turned his radio down and proceeded through the front door. Upstairs, Damon has his gun to Cash's head while Dirk has a gun to the back of Jaz's shoulder.

"Now what nigga?" Damon says to Dirk.

"Nigga I will kill this bitch… just like you did Max! I don't give a fuck!" Dirk yelled.

"Freeze mutha fucka… Savanna PD!" a male voice shouted coming from the stairs.

Damon turns to the sound of the voice. As he turns his back to Dirk, shots ranged out. Dirk shot Jaz in the back while Damon takes Cash head clean off, as he took cover. Attempting to grab Jaz from the chair, he was unsuccessful. Dirk and the cop fired at each other. Dirk hit Keyes in the shoulder throwing him from the landing. Damon fires at Dirk. The shots hit him in the stomach and once again in the chest.

Dirk went down emptying his mag. To no surprise, Damon was now standing above him. Dirk looks up at Damon and smiles. "You betta kill me muthafucka cuz you know I'm coming fo dat ass ag…" *Bang*! A shot between the eyes silenced him mid-sentence.

Damon immediately looks to Jaz who appeared to be dead, as blood swiftly was leaking from her chest. He calls out to her, "Jaz, Jaz!" She was unresponsive. Sirens seemed to come from everywhere now. Damon knew he needed to go and it was too late for goodbyes. He searches Dirks pockets for his keys. "Bingo!" he said, grabbing the keys as he heads downstairs and cautiously stepping over Keyes' limp body.

As officers arrive to the scene, they begin clearing the house. Upon seeing Officer Keyes on the landing, a call was placed. "Officer down!!! I repeat... officer down. Send a bus immediately to 1208 Lancaster Drive."

Keyes gasps and draws his weapon.

"Keyes! Damn it, its Hughes! Lower your weapon." Keyes tries to focus on the officer as he lowers his weapon.

"Jaz..." He worried.

"Is that the young lady upstairs?" Hughes asked. Keyes nodded. "I'll check; let's get you together first."

EMT's arrived and began working on Keyes.

Choices and Consequences

An officer from upstairs called for assistance. "We got a live one and she needs medical attention immediately! She lost a lot of blood." he adds.

Keyes hears the officer and snatches the IV out of his arm. Pushing past the EMT's, he forces his way up the stairs. Standing at the doorway he watched as they removed the duct tape from her body. Examining the room, he sees that Dirk and Cash are dead. However, there was no sign of Damon.

In the meantime, Damon was driving Dirks truck out of town. He didn't know where he was going; he just drove. He thought of Jaz and his unborn child, along with all the lies and deception that he had told and done; how it could have been prevented. He drove to a low-key motel where he often did business. Mr. Burns was the owner and he always let Damon pay cash. He never asked questions or gave any info.

"What's up Mr. B? I need a room for the night." Damon said, while placing $1,000 on the desk.

"No problem. Stay as long as you like." Mr. Burns added, as he handed Damon a room key in

121

exchange for the grand. Mr. Burns looks at the stack of cash. "One of those days, huh?" he said.

"Yeah one of those days... Goodnight Mr. B." Damon added, as he proceeded to his room.

Mr. Burns was a cool ass old man. He knew the business. In fact, he did his thang back in the day his damn self.

Damon took a shower and lie down to watch the news. There it was; his house all over the screen.

"Damn..." he mumbled. He did hear that an unidentified woman, along with Detective Keyes of Savanna PD survived the ordeal. That was a relief for Damon and he knew now he couldn't leave; not yet.

Chapter 13

Keyes sat in the hospital waiting for word about Jaz. An hour later a doctor came out informing him that Jaz had lost the baby but she would recover from her other wounds. It was a through and through wound. Keyes didn't know any relatives to contact nor did Jaz tell him about a baby. He was relieved to know she would recover. Keyes went in to see Jaz. Standing by her bed, he began to tear up. How could he fix this for her? Maybe he could somehow give her a reason to smile instead of cry.

Keyes sat at Jaz's bedside for the next couple of days. When she began to regain consciousness, she called out Damon's name. Startled, Keyes got up from his sleep. He gently grabbed her hand as he stood up.

"No… It's just me, Keyes." he spoke, with disappointment in his voice.

As her limp hand gripped his… "Keyes?" she questioned, as her eyes opened slightly. "My baby?" her voice low.

Keyes didn't know how to answer as he sighed "I'm sorry Jaz… the baby didn't make it. I'm so sorry."

He gripped her hand tighter as she began to cry out. Keyes sat down on the bed as he embraced her. It seemed as if all the hurt poured out of her. Keyes wanted to repair her heart.

Damon sat, as a million thoughts begin running through his mind. He needed to figure out a way to find out more info concerning Jaz. Knowing he couldn't call the hospital, he called in some favors. Scrolling through his phone, he saw the name Melissa Hogan. She was a former college buddy who was now a R.N. at Memorial University Medical Center.

He calls… "Emergency Department, Melissa speaking. How may I assist you?" she answered.

"What up doe Mel?"

"D... What's up? Long time, no hear from…" she whispers.

"Yeah, shit been kinda crazy. I know we need to catch up but right now I'm in desperate need of a favor."

"Hmmm, sounds a little risky considering you are all over the news." she said, in her bubbly voice.

"Well… you know. Special favors require special people, feel me?" he says, in his most charming voice.

"Soooo… This means you owe me huh?" she said blushing.

"No doubt… I gotchu."

"Okay D, what do you need?" she responds.

Explaining in as few words as possible, he requests the info he needs. After placing him on hold, she said to herself, "Damn right you owe me for this."

Looking up the aliases for recently checked in gunshot victims, she found a young black woman. Records indicated an exit wound through the left shoulder. Records also indicated loss of an embryonic fetus. Patient has 24 police detail and a no visitor mandate has been issued.

"Okay Damon, I have the info you need. So I'm calling in my favor now."

"Anything!" he said anxiously.

"Perfect. I know you seen that Lexus Coupe commercial right?"

He sighs, "Done."

"Sweet..." Mel added, as she gives him the info she just found.

Back in Jaz's room, Keyes attempts to hide his true feelings through the midst of the chaos. "Jaz, I know you're hurting cause I'm hurting for you. The truth is... you need rest. You are a strong, strong woman but this is far too much for anyone to deal with alone. Please allow me to help you. Anything you need just let me know. I'm right here." Jaz looks up at him with adoration in her eyes. She nodded as she eased her head into the pillow.

As Keyes exits the room, he spots a nurse. "Excuse me..." he gestures, as he proceeds to the nurses' station.

"Hold on a minute D." She puts the phone on the desk as she turns and sees Detective Keyes.

Desperately trying to keep her composure, she responds "Yes," in her voice normal.

"Ah Yes, I was wondering if I could trouble you for a cup of coffee."

Relieved, she replies, "Oh, it's no trouble at all. You look like you could use a cup; no offense." she adds jokingly.

"Yeah, it's been some long days."

"So are you waiting for your relief?" she inquires.

"Well no. I decided I'm going to stay. I guess you could say I have a personal interest in this case."

"Well of course, I saw the news. So are there any leads on the fugitive?" Mel probed, without any regard.

"Well, I'm afraid I can't discuss an open case," he responded with suspicion.

"Oh right… well let me handle this call and I'll bring your coffee."

"Okay thanks. I appreciate it." Keyes notices the name Reyes on the chart she was holding. He knew that was the alias given for Jaz.

"No problem." she says, as she waited for him to leave. Letting out a sigh relief, she returned to her call.

"Shit…" she whispered.

"My muthafuckin girl! See Mel dat's what I mean about special people; they handle dem delicate situations. You held me down and kept yo composure. I like dat. Now who is dis nigga wit da *personal interest* in the case?"

"That was Detective Keyes and between you and me, I think he's fucking the victim you're asking about," she whispers.

The next week seemed to be the longest of Damon's life. He was wondering if Jaz had been cheating while he was away. Maybe the baby wasn't his… maybe it was this punk ass nigga Keyes. Damon was going out of his mind with questions.

"Fuck it!" he said, as he texted Jaz's cell.

I'm sorry for everything. I'm sorry for getting you into this. I'm sorry for lying, and I'm sorry about your baby. Keyes sounds like he deserves you. I love you no matter what.

He sends the text. Immediately after, he lunges the cell phone towards the wall. The cell phone shatters into pieces.

Jaz reads the text. Immediately, her eyes fill with tears. Her heart ached. The love they shared still dwelt. Despite the fact that he lied and losing her unborn child that she so desperately wanted, how could he have the audacity to send a text like this? This was one helluva storm. Nana always said he don't bring us so far, to leave us. Jaz didn't feel that comfort. Tears formed in her eyes as she replied to Damon's text.

Why? He's only protecting me. You did this to me, our baby and our future. WTF! Goodbye.

Regrettably, Damon never replied.

Chapter 14

Weeks went by. "Ready?" Detective Keyes says walking in and pushing a wheelchair. She was being released finally. Jaz agreed to stay with Keyes until she found a new place with the money she had been saving. Keyes stayed in a quaint neighborhood, in which the streets were aligned with beautiful green trees. He lived in a two-bedroom Tudor style home. The landscape was stunning; red bushes, gorgeous blue flowers with a curve design made of pavement around them. Jaz loved the kitchen the most. It was decorated with a sub-zero fridge, chef style stove; white lacquer cabinets and gray stone counter tops. The rest of his place was equally lovely.

"Okay… I set the guest bedroom up for you. I'm sure it'll be more comfortable then that old hard ass hospital bed." He jokes, while he takes her things into the bedroom. Jaz sat down on the dark blue cloth sofa. Leaning back she closed her eyes. *'Now what, she thought to herself?'*

After months of recuperating, Jaz and Jason got closer. Jaz had turned over Taylors Haven to Ms. Kim. This was the start of her new life, which is what she wanted. Not hearing from Damon since that last text, she figured he was doing the same. Jaz felt so many different emotions when it came to Jason. He seemed to be everything any woman would want. He was tall, dark, and handsome with a good heart. He had that need to care for people. He was one of the good cops; that cop that you wanted in your corner when shit got bad.

Jaz was torn between Damon, the one who had her heart from the door, but turned her life upside down and Jason; the good guy who wanted to save her. She wanted her life to start over but her heart was still in the past. She could hear her Nana say don't let your past stop the blessings of your future.

Driving from a doctor's appointment, she got a call from Jason.

"Hey, Jason." she answered.

"Hey; so how was the visit?" he asked.

"It went well. The doctor said I can still have children."

"That's good news Jaz, good news. I'm happy for you."

"Yes it is… You know Jason; you have really been there for me. I just want to thank you. Words are just… not enough." she added, almost sad.

"Well, I'm here for you whenever you need me. Always remember that. I just called to check on you and I think I left a set of keys in your glove box. Can you check for me when you get time?" he added.

"I can do that for you now; hold on a sec." Jaz shuffles through papers and miscellaneous things in her glove box. She stumbles across a pink envelope addressed to her from Damon.

"No Jason; no keys here. Sorry."

"Okay, I'll keep looking. See you when I get home. Be safe." Jason hung up.

Closing her phone, Jaz stared at the envelope wondering what it could be. She took a deep breath before slowly opening it. There was a letter and a small silver key possibly to a safe. It read:

Dear Jaz,

If you are reading this, it means something went wrong. I guess this also means you found out that I was still in the game. I know I should've told you. Just know I did it for us; just know that. I did take precautions as far as finances. But knowing you, that doesn't matter at this point. Fidelity Bank, 260 Peachtree St., Atlanta GA. There is a box with your name on it. In it is a half a mill for you to do whatever it is you need to do. Whatever has happened, baby please know that I love you and always will; no matter what.

Loving You 4 Ever - No Matter What
Damon

Tears rolled down her face as she clenched the key and letter tightly to her chest. She cried out to Damon, as if he was sitting there. Yes, she was mad as hell and yes, she found out he was still in the game. Even still, her love for him didn't cease. Jaz felt alone and lonely, even though she knew she had Jason. He wasn't Damon. She proceeded to the address on the letter to collect what Damon had left.

After checking the box and transferring the funds to her personal account, she withdrew some money. She decided today was the day she would find her own place. Driving through the neighborhoods of Savanna, she looked for a place that was just right for her. After about 2 hours, she arrives at the place she knew she'd call home. The place was the Historic district of Savanna. She found a contemporary brown stone loft, located on Broughton Street. It was well within walking distance to River Street, Forsyth Park, galleries, restaurants, and all the downtown shopping. Immediately she walked in to get the info needed to rent one of the lofts and to look at a model.

She spoke with the owner of the building, Mr. Jensen. He informed her that today was her lucky day because he only had one left. The loft was newly renovated, with granite countertops, new stainless steel appliances, and had a modern chic décor; overlooking the main boutique shopping street in Savannah.

Jaz immediately wrote a check. Mr. Jensen welcomed her as he handed her the keys. It was on the second floor, so she took the stairs. She always took the stairs, even when elevators were present. It was her way of semi staying in shape. Inside, the high ceilings gave her a sense of openness, and the large ground to the ceiling windows let in an abundance of light to brighten the room. Antique hard wood floors completed the space.

It was partially furnished, with a king-size bedroom set, stove, fridge, washer, and dryer; along with central air.

She phoned Jason to explain the sudden move and he was okay with her getting on with her life. It's what he wanted for her. Only he wanted her to want it with him; nevertheless he was happy for her.

Once settled in, Jaz sat down with a hot cup of coffee. It could have been 100 degrees and she would still drink some coffee. Sitting on the ledge, she peered out the window at the hustle and bustle of the shoppers down below. The warm breeze sent the sweet smells of hot pastries from down the street through her nostrils. Closing her eyes, her mind drifted to the times when Damon would bring her hot doughnuts with her coffee in the morning. Then Jason came to mind. He was there when everything went to shit. She felt as if she owed him. She knew he felt something between them but she didn't share the same feelings; although she did care for him.

As the New Year approached, Jaz decided she'd cook a festive meal for the two of them. She hadn't spoken with Jason in a couple of days. Even though she had mixed feelings, she needed some companionship and Jason was the best thing for that. The fact is, Jaz missed him more than she was willing to admit to herself. As she reached for her cell, it began to ring. It was Jason. The caller ID read *Super Cop*; she smiled.

"Hey you, I was just bout to call you." Jaz spoke, her voice pleased.

"Yeah, yeah, yeah… You living the high life and forgot all bout' lil ole me, huh?" he responded. Jaz laughed.

"Not! It's not like that. You know you are my number one Super Cop."

"Oh, Super Cop huh? I like that." Jason was flattered. "So what's been going on… how's the new place and everything?"

"It's good. I love it. I just have to add my lil touches on it; you know a woman's touch is everything. "Thing is, I wanted to invite you over to see my place and cook us dinner if you weren't working on New Year's Eve." She added.

"Well, you know that will be a busy night... but I actually have it off. Is there anything I need to bring?"

"Just you; that's all I need." Jaz was surprised at the words that rolled off her tongue, as was Jason.

"Damn, I wasn't expecting that." Jason responded, feeling damn good right about now.

"Okay, you know I didn't mean it like that Jason." she laughs.

"Don't you mean Super Cop?" Jason retorts.

"Whatever... Just bring a bottle of Merlot; white preferably."

"I gotchu love. So what time are we talking 7... 8ish?"

"8 is good." she added, as they hung up.

Chapter 15

The next day Jaz figured she'd go out to shop for those womanly touches that she had mentioned. She drove till she arrived at Georgia furniture and interiors. A long time ago, Ms. Kim had mentioned this place to her. Walking in, the store was filled with wall-to-wall furniture for every room. A salesperson greeted her, Jaz glances over the showroom and ran down a list of things she needed. He was all too happy to get her everything on her list. He knew this was a big ticket and a big commission for him. After about 3 hours in the store, Jaz had gotten everything for her new place and even a few extras. Now it was time to go shopping for plants, dishes and such.

After two more hours, she got that out of the way and did some clothes shopping too; along with a little grocery shopping. Jaz was now exhausted and hungry as hell. She stops by a Mickey D's and ordered a number 1.

Afterward, she headed home to put the groceries away and called it a night.

The next morning was New Year's Eve. Jaz put the added touches on her new place, as she waited for the arrival of her furniture. She was excited and a little anxious about Jason coming over. As she placed her new dishes in the cabinet, her mind drifted back to when Damon showed her the new house that he'd bought for them. She remembered how excited she was then.

Meanwhile… Damon was back gathering as much Intel as he could on Detective Keyes. He knew Keyes was the closest thing to finding Jaz. Damon also made good on his promise to Mel… A Lexus Coupe that was candy apple red, with tan guts that Damon picked himself. Mel was ecstatic and she loved it, even if Damon had one of his boys drop it off to her. She knew the deal.

Jason was home getting ready for his dinner with Jaz. He too was anxious and excited. Jason showered and shaved; splashing on a hint of Bvlgari cologne. Pulling out his black and silver Armani suit, he decided to omit the jacket. The vest was black with silver pinstripes, as were his slacks. His white button up matched perfectly, along with his black and silver tie and diamond cuff links. He topped it off with a black band Bvlgari watch. He was definitely dressed to impress.

Jaz hadn't cooked like this in a long time. It reminded her of Nana and her New Year's recipes that she cooked every year. Jaz was the only person she ever told her secret recipe to. '*Just put a lil sugar in it.*' is what Nana always said when it came to cooking. The collard greens were just about done and so was the baked macaroni. The sweet smell of honey-baked ham filled the loft. It was topped with cherries and pineapples. Hawaiian sweet rolls were last on the agenda. The strawberry pie she baked the night before sat nice and chill in the fridge. It was time to shower with her favorite strawberry-scented body wash.

Jason drew stares as he walked thru the House of Liquor.

"What's going on Unc?" he said to the cashier.

"Nephew! He yelled joyfully. "You sayin' som'n ain't ya? Where da party at?"

"Now you know I ain't the one for partying Unc. It's just a lil one on one thing. I need the best White Merlot you got."

"You ain't said nuddin' but a word. Which one you want? I got Gallo, Beringer, Sutter Home, that shit in the box but you dressed too sharp for that. Here, take the Beringer nephew; it's on me. Happy New Year to ya!"

"Same to you Unc. I really appreciate it. Be safe and lock up a lil early. You know how these fools get." Keyes exits.

Damon sat outside a few cars back, watching as Keyes entered his jet-black Durango. As he pulled off, so did Damon, making sure he stayed at least three cars behind. *'It's on.'*

Still wet from the shower, Jaz walked into the kitchen wrapped in a towel. She removed the macaroni from the oven and replaced it with the dinner rolls; setting them on warm. Proceeding back to the bedroom she pulled out a Black embellished Jimmy Choo cocktail dress. The sides were aligned with diamond studs, along with matching Jimmy

142

Choo 6 inch heels. She smiles at the thought of Jason seeing her dressed up. After getting lotion up, she used spritz and a hint of J'adore perfume along her arms legs, neck and back. She grabs a matching black lingerie set that she'd bought from Fredrick's of Hollywood.

Jaz stood in front of the floor length mirror. Smoothing out her dress and slipping on her heels, she smiled. "You are looking fierce girl!" she said to herself. She proceeded to pull out the dinner rolls and set the table. Black and Silver decorated the table; down to the napkins and plates. Centering the table was a silver metal pail full of ice. Now it was time to set the mood with one of her favorite artists; Maxwell. She set the CD player to repeat the entire Urban Suite CD. (*BUZZ BUZZ*) Jaz breathed a deep breath, looked at her watch and buzz the buzzer. She knew it had to be Jason. Opening the door Jason inhaled and exhaled with a smile across his face. "Damn!" he shouted, as he covers his mouth with his fist.

"I take it you like..." Jaz laughed, as she extended a hand to invite him in.

"Wow is all I can say," he added, as he walked into her place.

"Looking good… damn and you smell extra good." Jason leans in to draw in her scent.

Jaz closes the door while retrieving the bottle of wine from his hand. "Thank you. Please make yourself comfortable." she added, as she went into the kitchen to search for a corkscrew. "I must say Jason, you are lookin' damn good yourself… nice change from the uni." She laughs, referring to his every day work attire.

"Well thank you… I think… why you getting on my uni? It's my Colombo outfit." He laughed, placing the bottle in the ice pail and retrieving the corkscrew from her.

"No, it's not like that. I love the uni… it's just you know this… this is hot!" she pointed to his man wear.

"Okay, okay… how hot I like… I guess that gets you off the hook." They both laughed. "You hooked the place up. I see you added womanly touches." Jason said, as he walked around the loft briefly.

"Oh yeah, you know. I had to put a lot of me into this place… but now I love it and I'm glad you like it." She headed back to the kitchen and began fixing their plates. Jason came in behind her. "Wow, you really did your thing, huh?" he admired her cooking skills.

"Of course! Nana taught me well… But you need to go have a seat and let me play hostess." she gently nudged him out the kitchen.

"I can do that and pour wine." They laughed as Jason poured the wine and sat down at the table. He couldn't keep his eyes off her. Each time she came to the table, her thigh length dress showed off her reddish brown thick thighs. When she turned to walk away was even a better view. Her dress hugged her ass and hips to a t. Jaz soon sat down. "You okay?" she inquired, as to his quietness.

"Yeah I am okay. I'm just thinking; a New Year and so much has happened?" he added.

"Yeah… I know, but I will say this… I am so grateful for my many blessings and for you." Jaz looked at him. Her eyes were sincere and emotional.

"Me?" he was surprise and gratified.

"May I say Grace?" he asked.

145

"Yes you... I mean you have been with me from the day that I met you and for that alone I am so grateful Jason." Tears began forming in her eyes. Jason reached across the table, caressing her right hand.

"I will always be here for you." he expressed, as he dabbed her tears with his forefinger.

"I know in my heart you mean that... you are too good to me." she smiled.

"You deserve it all Jaz and hopefully one day you'll choose me to give it to you." he added. Jason knew he loved her but he also knew she didn't love him the way he needed her to. Nevertheless, he was patient and she was worth waiting for.

"May I?" Jason added, as he looked down at the table.

"Of course..." she said reaching for his other hand. Jason said Grace. They ate, talked and drank wine throughout dinner. That lasted at least 2 hours. *'This was much needed.'* Jaz thought to herself, looking across the table. This man was perfect for her in every sense of the word. Thoughts of Damon tried to creep into her mind but she wouldn't hear of it. She would block them out, at least for tonight.

Jason deserved to have all her attention. Suddenly a loud bang ranged out. "Jason!" she screams, as she headed to the floor. Jason laughed, catching Jaz before she hit the floor.

"No Jaz… It's just the fireworks show they are doing in the park. "They do it every year. You've lived so far in the suburbs before sweetheart, now you're in the city." he laughs, helping her back to her chair.

"Oh, my God! I know, right?" she tried to calm herself. Jason poured them another glass of wine. "Let me show you what all the noise is really about." He led Jaz over to the window. "Look, you can see it real good from here." he hugged Jaz from behind, as they watched the firework show and sipped their wine. *BOOM, BOOM*!

Beautiful colors and shapes lit up the sky.

"It is beautiful… and loud as hell." she said.

"Yea it is," he responded. He was looking down at her; feeling her ass push against him every time she jumped or shivered. Jason could feel himself getting aroused, so he stepped back just enough for her not to notice, as he regained his composure. The show lasted about 30 minutes. Once over, they sat on the peach leather couch that sat in front of that very window. They watched the show from it and didn't even realize that Jaz had nestled herself against Jason's shoulder. They cuddled on the couch in silence for a few moments. Jason closed his eyes, as did Jaz; both feeling too relaxed. "I love you Jaz!" Jason whispers. Jaz opened her eyes at the words that she'd just heard. Slowly, she sat up.

"You love me?" she questioned, as if she didn't know he felt this way. Maybe she just needed to hear him say it again. Jason cleared his throat and opened his eyes.

"Yes, I love you Jaz and have for a long time now... I felt something for you the day you walked into my office. For the life of me, I couldn't explain it to you or myself." he confessed. Without words, Jaz pulls him toward her and gently kissed his lips. There had been so many nights that he could only imagine feeling the softness of her lips. He'd even imagine feeling what her body felt like against his or her allowing him to pleasure her. He could feel the arousal building inside him.

"Make love to me Jason." she moaned, giving him full range of her open mouth. Their tongues danced together, as their voices moaned together.

Chapter 16

Jaz gradually climbed on Jason's lap, without breaking their kiss. His hands squeezed the softness of her ass as she moaned a little louder. Jason wanted Jaz at this moment but he also wanted this to be a stained memory in both of their minds and hearts. His left hand, bit by bit, unzipped the back of her zipper and revealed the black lingerie. Smoothly he broke their kiss. "What's wrong?" her voice soft and sensuous.

"Nothing… I just wanta look at you." he responded, sounding almost sad. She smiled as she stood giving him full view. More and more he could see virtually every curve and dip along her body. His groin was pulsating to the point where he needed to re-adjust himself. Jaz unbuttoned her bra from the front, as her round breast bounced as they were freed. Jason gasped. He couldn't wait any longer. He needed to touch her to feel her and she knew it. Sliding her black lace panties down in one slow motion she stood before him exposed. *'Her beauty is breath taking.'* he thought. She reached for his hand and he obliged. She could lead him to hell if she wanted to and he'd go. Jaz led him to the bedroom. Her ass swung from side to side, with just enough bounce.

Once in the bedroom room she turns and begins to undress him. Taunting her nipples with each hand, this gave her an intense sensation within her. Once her task was completed, she stood back to admire the view before her. *'Damn! He is hung like a stallion.'* she thought, with a wicked smile; one-eye brow up - one down.

"To your satisfaction?" he asked. He knew he was holding the goods.

"Yes, I know you were knocking down in yo day…" she said, as her hands stroked his abs.

"I wouldn't say all that. I was a little selfish with myself." he added.

As he picked Jaz up, she wrapped her legs around his waist. Again, they explored each other's

152

mouths. Jason soon took one of her nipples into his warm wet mouth; slightly biting.

"Jason…" she whimpered.

Careful to give each nipple what it deserved, his hands cuffed her ass cheeks; squeezing them as his fingers came so close to her pussy that he could feel the slippery substance oozing from her.

Jason slid Jaz down until her feet touched the floor. "Sit on my face!" sounding as if he was outta breath. She indulged him. Lying down on his back, Jaz climbed over him holding on to the headboard.

He squeezed her soft ass once again, before sliding his tongue in an up and down motion against her clit. Her back immediately went into an arch as she cried out his name. He continued, as his strokes got more and more intense; she rocked back and forth on his face.

"Jason, I'm cumm…"

"Give it to me then…" he mumbles, now sucking at her juices as they gushed forth.

Once her rhythm slowed, he eased from up under her, wiping his face and ready. She dropped to the bed and rolled over on her back. That first one had taken a lot from her but it was long past due, since she hadn't been masturbating much. Jason leaned over her.

"Are you okay?" he grins.

"Yea... I'm so okay." she giggled, hinting that she was ready for more. Jason embraces the soft smooth skin surrounding her nipples. "I need to feel you." she moans softly, while pulling him closer. Jason almost immediately began easing his hardness inside her, inch by inch, making sure she wasn't uncomfortable with his size. She wasn't. Wrapping her legs around his waist, once more her pc muscles began pulling him.

"Awww... Jaz!" "Damn baby," he hums. As he thrusts deeper inside her, gushing noises release from her pussy. Feeling like he was tapping the bottom of her insides, she moaned louder and louder while calling out his name. This excited him even more. "Oooo, you bout to make me cum... wait I don't want to; not yet... shit I can't hold it Jaz!" Jason almost shouted. Jaz pc muscles squeezed harder as her hips rose to meet his. It was over. She felt herself cumming again. She grabs his forearms, as her breasts bounce with each hard thrust he delivers. He felt her juices exploding on the tip of his dick and he exploded with her.

Meanwhile, Damon sat in his car contemplating what he was going to do. So many thoughts poison his mind. He felt confused and outraged with the thought of Jaz being with anyone but him. Blinking his eyes, he attempted to get the visual of Jaz and Keyes fucking. Suddenly, he jumped out of his car and placed his gun in the back of his jeans. He went to the building, scanning the mail boxes, until he found Jaz's last name.

"I gotcha!" He pointed to her apartment number with a wicked smirk.

He headed back to his car. Sitting for a few more moments he looked down at his watch and saw that it was 2:55 a.m. He couldn't and wouldn't wait any longer. *'This nigga ain't spendin' the night tonight.'* he thought to himself, as he exited his car.

Noticing a chick walking up to the building, he asks her to hold the door for him. After looking back at Damon, who was fine no matter how rough he looked, she was pleased to do so. "Thank you Sweetheart. Damn... you looking good tonight!

Where da party at?" he was smooth wit it. She laughs a cute laugh.

"I'm done partying but if you wanta come up I'm in 312. My name is Shay."

"Oh, ok Shay. I might take you up on that later." he smiled, trying to hurry.

"Yea, you do that wit yo fine ass." she added, as she proceeded to the elevator. Damon started jogging down the hall to the other end where elevators were also present for the second floor. She turned to see if he was watching her but he wasn't. That's when she noticed the gun in the back of his jeans. Instantaneously, she turns away while hurrying to her elevator that had opened.

Once in her own apartment, she called the super and told him that there was a strange man in the hall with a gun, but she didn't know what floor he was on. She figured she'd better get the hell outta there since this guy knew where she lived. The super called his son Hughes, also a police officer and a colleague of Jason. After explaining what the woman had told him, he hung up and peered out the window. He was looking for any signs of a strange looking man lurking about.

Choices and Consequences

A loud knock at the door abruptly awakened Jaz and Jason. "What the fuck!" Jason startled, as he jumps up. Jaz sits up. "You expecting anybody?" he asks. Jaz shook her head. "Ms. Taylor... this is Shay. I just wanted to use your phone." Shay's voice was low. Damon had caught her coming from her apartment and had her at gunpoint. "Oh, that's one of the ladies from in the building... I'll get it." Jaz laughed at her own nervousness. Putting on her robe, she headed for the door. As she went to peek through the peep hole, the loud knock again caused her to jump back. This pissed her off. *'This bitch coming to my door wee hours of the morning and gon knock like she da police. She must be crazy!'* Jaz thought, as she swung open the door. "Damon!" she cried out! Suddenly, Damon pushed Shay into the apartment as he locked the door behind him and grabbed Jaz in the process.

Jason runs into the living room. "Damon... you gotta lot of balls boy!" Jason smirked. Damon ignored Jason for a moment, as he held Jaz in front of him with his gun in her side. Opening her robe, he saw that she was naked. He looked at Jason and

157

then back at Jaz. Damon's free hand went between Jaz's legs. "No Damon, please!" she began to cry.

"Hey man! What da fuck is dat all about?" Jason walked toward Damon.

"Don't be stepping mutha fucka!" Damon pointed the gun at Jason, as he held onto Jaz his arm now around her neck. He smelled his hand. "You fuck dis nigga... didn't you?" he shouted. Jaz said nothing as she continued to cry. No answer would be good enough and she knew that. "Listen, I don't know anybody here, so please just let me go and I won't say shit!" Shay begged. "Bitch you sit and shut the fuck up!" he waved the gun toward her and back at Jason.

"Damon, what kinda life you think she gon have with you... always on the run, always looking over shoulder; you think maybe she been through enough?" Jason tried to reason with Damon. It worked to a point as Damon pushed Jaz back towards Jason.

"Dats where you wanna be right?" he said.

"Damon, with everything that has happened do you think for a minute I want to have a life on the run?" Jaz cried.

"It was cool when we came here hiding from that Dirk; keeping you safe and shit!" Damon's head moved back and forth, as he got angry again. "Let me ask you… whose baby was it?" Damon waited.

"Whose baby… nigga that baby was-"

"Nigga shut the fuck up… I'm talking to her." Damon interrupted, while pointing the gun toward Jaz.

"It was yours Damon… yours!" Jaz wept. Jason tried to comfort her as Damon watched in disgust.

"You know what? Fuck dat! Get yo ass back over here!" Damon commanded.

"Damon, you not getting her back…" Jason held onto Jaz.

"Nigga, I will kill her before I let her be wit you… shit neither of us will have her… you want dat!" Damon yelled. "Get over here now Jaz or I may just kill this nigga… yo choice!" he added infuriated.

Jaz slowly began to move toward Damon. She knew he would kill somebody in that room.

"Jaz; you don't have to do this." Jason pleaded. Jaz didn't respond. When she got closer to Damon he snatched her even closer.

"Damon, please!" she pleaded.

"Don't worry; we gon be alrite… you'll see. Im'a take care of you." Damon's voice calm. This scared the shit outta Jaz. Shay tried to ease toward the kitchen. Damon stepped back while still holding on to Jaz and fired one shot. It hit Shay in the stomach. He then aimed the gun directly towards Jason. Jason didn't get a chance to do anything but take one step.

"I told yo ass don't be a hero nigga… now you pissing me off once again!" Damon yelled.

He was so mad now and his blood was boiling. Jason stood there. He didn't move back. Shay laid on the floor whimpering.

Suddenly, a loud knock was at the door surprising Damon. "Savanna PD! Open the door!" a male voice spoke.

Jason knew it was Hughes voice. Damon looked at the door and Jason lunged at him at exactly at the same time. Jaz dropped to the floor and ran over to Shay. They tussled over the gun. Jaz screams. Hughes had an officer hit the door with a battering ram. Shots rang out for what seemed like a matter of minutes.

Shots rang out as soon as the door flew open. When it was all said and done, Jaz's lifeless body laid draped over Shay; who was alive but passed out. A single gunshot to Jaz's chest killed her instantly. Damon was wounded in the shoulder and Keyes was untouched. Later, Damon was charged with the death of Jazmine Taylor, along with other numerous accounts. In the end, Damon was right; neither of them would have her. Damon would sit in the Georgia State Prison to think about the events that led up to this, including his undying love for Jaz and the hatred that streamed through his blood. Nana always said to be careful of the choices you make in life, because just like cause and effect, there are consequences to our choices.

The End

About the Author

L. Hunter is a wonderful and patient mother of five. She is a native of Detroit, Michigan and has been writing since the year 2000. When L. Hunter was very young her grandmother started her off reading the newspaper. Every since then she has loved reading and writing. With *Choices and Consequences*, L. Hunter wants her readers to come away with the causes and effects of choices we make in everyday life. Another passion she wants for her readers is just to enjoy her books. *Choices and Consequences* is only the beginning. Look for more books coming from L. Hunter.

Connect with Author L. Hunter:
authorlhunter@gmail.com
www.facebook.com/LaShonKapriHunter